Mirror of Danger

A Gripping Mystery Suspense

A Jessica Smith
Book 3

Ava S. King

Latest Releases: Ava S. King

Agent Red Series

Fatal Memory Teagan Stone Book 1
Fatal Target Teagan Stone Book 2
Fatal Crime Teagan Stone Book 3
Fatal Justice Teagan Stone Book 4
Fatal Enemy Teagan Stone Book 5
Fatal Death Teagan Stone Book 6
Fatal Revenge Teagan Stone Book 7
Fatal Pursuit Teagan Stone Book 8
Fatal Attack Teagan Stone Book 9

Jessica Smith Series

Mirror of Lies -A Jessica Smith Book 1
Mirror of Lust -A Jessica Smith Book 2
Mirror Of Danger -A Jessica Smith Book 3

Upcoming Releases

Christina Harris- Thriller, Suspense Book 1
Agent Red Fatal Mission Teagan Stone Book 10
Restored: Book 2

Introduction

Sign-up to Ava S. King's mailing list for news, new releases and special offers.

www.authoravasking.com

Disclaimer

A work of fiction contains strong language and explicit content and is only intended for mature readers. The story may contain unconventional situations, language, and sexual encounters that may offend some readers. This book is for mature readers (18+).

Synopsis

Jessica returned to work after the kidnapping and the death of her best friends. Now it was time to go back full time as a journalist and put her mind on the job. It only made sense when a story dropped in her lap to continue finding out what the police had missed. The biggest story across the news stations caused her to not only be the face in the media, but someone had other plans that derailed her into danger.

Can Jessica put her life back on track once again?

Chapter One

Standing in front of the Bengal College library, Carolyn waited for her best friend to meet her. They were headed to the local pizza shop to grab pizza. A soft woman at five six, Carolyn has a rich fawn like beauty. It was a Friday night at eight when they made plans after her latest tutoring session with the top basketball player on campus. The past week had been frustrating with wanting to find a second job because her financial aid wasn't enough to cover all her bills. Alyssa waved as she approached Carolyn at the front steps and they hugged.

"How was the tutoring session?" Alyssa asked, and fell into step with Carolyn.

Carolyn shrugged, then gripped her book bag. She held onto her keys, headed down the walkway to the parking section, and unlocked the doors to her car. They'd been best friends for over ten years and Alyssa was on the taller side at five seven, with shoulder length brunette hair and an athletic build.

"Same thing as usual. He's trying to flirt and I was

trying to work." Carolyn rolled her eyes thinking back on Harper trying to get her number. She's the type of girl he wouldn't normally go for if he saw her out with his friends. Carolyn liked to read, watch movies, and knit in her spare time. Harper was the basketball star, and partying type who stayed in drama on campus. As the popular jock on campus, he was known as a womanizer, but his reputation never prevented women from flirting with him, until Carolyn.

"You're a junior in college. You need to have fun," Alyssa said, then locked her seatbelt around her waist.

Carolyn slid the key in the ignition. She turned the headlights on, reversed backwards to drive around to the front of the school, and headed toward the main road.

"I have a lot to do." Carolyn drove slowly out of the student parking area, and turned the radio on to her favorite R&B station when out of the corner of her eye she saw a crowd of people running to the front area, crying together in a huddle.

She pointed at the commotion. "What's that?"

"Not sure, pull over," Alyssa stated. Carolyn normally didn't get involved in any drama, but it was weird to see people running toward the action. She moved to an open spot and placed the car in park with it still running. Alyssa jumped out and walked over to a group of people. Carolyn saw Alyssa cover her mouth in shock, then someone leaned in to give her a hug. Carolyn's brow hiked in curiosity. A few seconds went by and Alyssa approached her car again and dipped her head in the window.

"What's wrong. Why are you crying?" Carolyn probed.

Alyssa blew out a breath. She closed her eyes, trying to hold back tears. "It happened again, Carolyn."

"What?"

"Jocelyn the RA is dead," Alyssa said, and Carolyn gasped in surprise. Jocelyn Gambit the residential assistant at the college. Even though she didn't live on campus, she liked Jocelyn and felt comfortable talking with her about her goals and dreams. As they talked, an ambulance arrived and Carolyn turned the car off and slid out to see what was happening.

"Do they know how she died?" Carolyn asked.

"No, but it's crazy to have two deaths in the same year on campus," Alyssa murmured and Carolyn locked her arm with Alyssa in comfort.

* * *

Ellen planted her hands on her hips. "When are you going to have the story on my desk, Jessica?"

Jessica was so startled by the sound of Ellen's booming voice, she popped up from her sleep and sat straight up. She pushed her hair back out of her face.

Ellen stood at the conference room table and stared into her eyes. "I don't pay you to sleep." Monday morning came fast and she'd just gotten back from her vacation after visiting family and friends back home. Her flight came in late and she still needed to be at work to show everyone that she wasn't some fragile reporter who ran away from home. The last few years had been a roller coaster for Jessica and she was wiser, with her head on straight. Sometimes she felt people were staring at her and wanted to ask how she really was doing after being kidnapped, especially her coworkers. To them, it was another story, but for Jessica, it was her life that had been put in harm's way.

Jessica stretched her arms wide and yawned. "Sorry, my flight came in late last night." She turned the computer on and logged into her emails.

"Did you hear anything I said in the meeting?"

"Yeah," Jessica lied. They both scanned her notepad and it was blank.

"Jessica, you wanted to be treated like everyone else, so I expect you to be on it at the office."

"Ellen, you know I love my job."

Jessica couldn't blame Ellen for her still being off and not in her head sometimes. Her work had slacked for the past few months, but she promised to get back on her game. *The Gazette* was a major news brand that anyone would be proud to work for and she was letting her past come between her present and the future.

Ellen tapped her finger on top of the table, walked out of the room. "Show me because since everything has happened, you've lacked in your writing."

Jessica took the notepad, flipped it over and stood up. She sauntered out of the office to the break room and picked up the coffee pitcher, removed a cup and filled her glass. The only thing on her mind was light and fluffy stories -- nothing that sparked her interest to bring back her gut feelings. Jessica filled the steamy mug with her favorite creamer and one sugar packet. After blowing on the cup she took that first precious sip and smiled. She was trekking back down the hall from the break room when she was flagged down by her co-worker.

"How'd the meeting go?" Rowan asked, with his feet cocked up on his desk. Jessica shrugged, then leaned over his desk to glance at the newspaper.

Jessica lifted the paper in her hand and read the head-line. "Fine."

Rowan's brows creased together. "Based on your mood it went sour."

"She's pissed I fell asleep in the meeting."

He burst into laughter.

Jessica smacked him on the arm with the newspaper. "Not funny, Rowan."

"Ellen won't get rid of you, not her star reporter."

Everyone at the Gazette knew Jessica was the top reporter they wanted to be. Nothing was off-limits when she pitched a story. Higher-ups let her get away with things a junior reporter wouldn't normally get away with.

Jessica turned the newspaper around to face him. "Nice piece on the climate issues at the factory," Jessica said, and placed the newspaper back down on the desk.

"Thanks. What are you working on?"

Jessica turned to saunter into her office. "Nothing."

"Only a matter of time before something falls in your lap," Rowan called to her back. Jessica pushed her door open and was surprised to find Leo sitting at her desk.

She looked over her shoulder, then closed the door. She popped her hand on her hip. "Leo."

Leo sat forward in her chair.

Jessica stepped closer. She planted a hand on the edge of the chair and placed her cup down. "What are you doing here?"

"I need your help."

Jessica squinted her eyes and came around to her desk. He jumped up from the desk and she sat down in the empty chair and dropped her notepad. "My help?"

Leo plopped down in the chair. "A possible serial killer."

Jessica lifted her pen. She flipped open her notebook. "Where?"

"Bengal College."

Jessica froze and closed the notebook. "I can't help you." Fear filled her eyes.

His eyes rose in surprise. "You didn't hear me out."

Jessica sighed and closed her eyes for a minute. She flickered them open and stared up at Leo. "Listen, I have too much work already," she complained, throwing her hands up in the air.

"Since when do you not take on more than one story?"

Jessica shrugged her shoulders. "Sorry, Leo. Find someone else."

Leo picked up the folder and handed it to her. Jessica stared at his hand and pulled it from him.

"Read it and let me know what you think." Leo whirled around and walked out of her office.

Jessica yelled at his back, "I'm busy, Leo!" She groaned and covered her face in her hands.

Whenever anyone forced her to do anything, it only made her more annoyed and angry. Leo never cared and just continued to ignore her attitude. Years of friendship made him know her moods.

She thought her time of being reminded about Bengal College would be over after she left years ago. Somehow her past and her future had finally collided. Jessica clicked the top of the pen in her hand on and off and stared down at the folder.

"You can just look at the notes. Jessica... doesn't mean you agree."

Jessica flipped it open and stared at the first picture of a young brown haired girl who looked no more than twenty-six, full lips, chesnut skin tone. Jessica went to Bengal College in the beginning of her journey, but an incident at a college party turned her world upside down. One night out with her friends was supposed to be a fun way to burn off some steam. She never expected to be almost attacked. Jessica closed the folder and leaned back in her chair. With a heavy sigh, she pressed her hands on the back of her head and glanced up at the ceiling. A knock sounded on her door, but she zoned out as the knock continued.

The door pushed open to Ellen. "Hey, you didn't catch what I was saying?"

Jessica sat forward. "Oh, sorry. What did you say?"

Ellen came inside, shut the door and laid her back against the door. "Are you alright?"

"Yeah, fine." Jessica smiled but the smile felt forced.

"Are you really up to being back full time?"

Jessica pulled up her white linen shirt on her wrists. "Come on, Ellen, you've asked me this a million times."

"And I will ask you a million and one. Jessica, you've gone through some traumatic events." Ellen looked at her with something fragile in her eyes.

Jessica rubbed a hand down her face. "I promise I will let you know if I need a break."

She stared at Jessica for another second before speaking. "I need you on the Bengal College case."

"Wait, I have a story already."

Ellen was the boss Jesscia wanted to avoid when she came onboard because sometimes it was a tug of war to get on the same page with her. Both were stubborn. Jessica felt like she brought the readers in with her reporting, while Ellen felt Jessica needed to be more well-rounded and less pushy in her stories.

"I will have someone else run it. You're on this story today."

"But-"

Ellen held her hand up to stop her from speaking. "Unless there's a reason you can't work on the story."

Jessica was too scared to speak up and just shook her head. She gathered her thoughts and said, "Fine, I can cover the story."

"Good. See what you can get from Leo."

Jessica raised the folder in her hand. "On it already."

"That's from Leo?" she questioned.

"Yep, first thing on the agenda. He dropped it off." Jessica knew she wouldn't be able to hold back the floodgates of black memories from that time of her life. Though she believed she had pushed them away forever, she knew she was wrong.

"Go interview her family, friends, and school professors."

Jessica threw up her thumb in the air. "On it, boss," she sarcastically responded.

Her editor chuckled, tossed her blissfully blond hair back and strode away, leaving her alone again.

Jessica clicked on her computer searching for the latest information for Bengal College, moving through each day of the past few weeks. Over and over she'd come up with the same information of the young girl doing the same routine of going from class to spending time with her friends.

"Talk to me, Jocelyn."

Jessica picked up her phone and ordered breakfast to be delivered and sat back watching the news articles discussing Joceyln's death and the family's heartbreak.

* * *

Jessica removed her glasses and wiped the tiredness from her eyes. She was exhausted from a long day of running over file notes, researching Joceyln's background, and her last few days at school. Jessica turned off her computer, scooted back in her chair, stood up and grabbed all of her notes. She tossed the case folder in her bag and reached for her purse and keys, then turned the light off and ambled away from her desk and headed home. An hour later Jessica dragged her feet inside, hanging her coat on the rack in her apartment. She kicked off her shoes, ambled to the night table and pressed the red button, checked her answering machine and walked to the fridge.

"*Hey, Jessica. It's Leo. Call me tomorrow so we can meet up.*"

Another voice message from her mother. "*Hi, sweetie. It's your mom. Call me. I miss your face.*"

Jessica scooped up a fork, removed the lid on the container of the Chinese food she had taken from the fridge and marched into her bedroom. She turned on the tv to decompress before showering and going to bed. A best friend came into the room and purred. She'd gotten the cat from animal rescue, her white and black fur melted against her touch as she jumped on the bed and rubbed the top of her head. Before she could let her ponytail down, her phone rang. Jessica huffed and jogged to her purse for her phone.

Jessica held the phone to her ear. "Hello."

"Help me." A low whimpering sound cascaded through the phone.

Jessica pulled the phone away from her ear. "Hello? Who is this?"

"Please you have to help me," the same soft voice whispered urgently.

Jessica searched around the room for a pen and paper. "Tell me your name."

"Oh god, he's coming." A sob escaped.

The call disconnected. Jessica's brow squinted in confusion and she held the phone up to check the number. The display read unknown.

"Who was that?"

Not able to get the call off her mind she tried to redial and it announced as disconnected and unknown name. As she got back to her bedroom she placed her phone on the charger and dialed Leo's number, listening to it ring.

"*You've reached Leo Walsh. I can't come to the phone right now.*"

Jessica groaned and tossed the phone back on the stand, curled up with her cat and picked up her food to continue eating.

"Was that Jocelyn? Or another girl in trouble?" Jessica mumbled, once she finished eating. Jessica strolled to the bathroom, put her hair up and turned the shower on and waited for the steam to fill the room. She prayed the girl would call back and she could get more information.

Ring!

Jessica poked her head out of the bathroom at the sound of her phone going off and ran to pick it up. "Hello."

"You called me," Leo's groggy voice spoke.

"Yeah, are you sleeping?"

"What do you think, Jess?"

Jessica cut her eyes to the clock on the nightstand reading one am. "Sorry to bother you. It can wait."

"Are you sure?"

Jessica didn't want to alarm him; it was probably a prank call, so she went with her gut to hold off until she knew more.

"Positive. See you tomorrow."

"Goodnight, Jess."

"Goodnight, Leo."

After showering she fell into bed, not able to sleep as she thought whoever spoke on the other end of the call needed serious help. Ellen might have been right about her taking on the story. She'd thought about talking with a therapist, to work through what had happened in her past. She realized bringing more awareness to women being kidnapped could shine a light on a big issue.

Chapter Two

The barber trimmed his beard and sideburns just the way he liked them. Cedric finished his work for the day and wanted to run a few errands. Over the past few weeks he had been working nonstop to get his project at school finished and turned in, on top of being a teacher's assistant and preparing for finals. Trying to have a social life had left him with little to no time. Everyone he had come across was only interested in the bad boy or guy with loads of money. Cedric felt his looks were average, but decent as a six-one guy, with dark brown curls, broad shoulders, and a slim build. Growing up he wasn't the biggest sports person, but he was still muscular in certain areas even though he had a slim build. Cedric waited for his barber to turn the chair around after wiping his face with a warm towel. He slipped his hand in his pocket and removed a few bills to pay and stood shaking his hand.

"Same time again in two weeks," his barber stated.

"As always," Cedric remarked. He strolled through the exit and out of the building, and hit the alarm on his car and hopped in. He turned the ignition and placed the car in reverse. Cedric twisted the knob on the radio, listening to the news channel.

"We have reports of Jocelyn Gambit's remains being found. Funeral arrangements being set by her family," the radio host announced.

Cedric tuned them out and swerved into the nearby parking space of the burger spot close to campus. He climbed from his seat and locked his door. He waved at a few students, pulled the door wide to let them in first, and smiled.

"Cedric, are you giving out the answers to the next quiz?" a young redhead, wearing shorts and a crop top asked.

"Leah, you know I can't do that."

"Bummer. I was looking forward to having a private study session." Leah grinned, and grasped hold of her friend's hand and switched off. Cedric shook his head and made it up to the front of the line and glanced at the menu on the board.

"I'm so serious, Carolyn. Once we finish studying we should send flowers to her parents," Alyssa explained.

Carolyn held her wallet and took her bank card out, ready to pay. "You are right. Jocelyn's family finally got closer, so it should be fine to go visit," Carolyn responded, then removed her shades.

Cedric froze in place at their words.

"Next in line!" the cashier yelled.

Cedric hadn't moved.

"I think lilies were her favorite," Alyssa stated.

"Next in line!" the cashier repeated.

Carolyn pressed a hand to Cedric's shoulder and he whipped around in a sneer.

Alyssa pointed.

"You're next," Carolyn said.

"Oh, I must have zoned out," Cedric suggested, laughing with the girls.

"Aye, aren't you the teacher's assistant at Bengal College?" Alyssa probed.

Cedric moved up to the window. "I am." He faced the cashier. "Can I get the mega combo and a Sprite, please." After he placed his order, Cedric took a twenty from his back pocket.

Alyssa winked at Carolyn and she blushed. "I thought I recognized you."

"That will be nine-forty-five," the cashier said, grabbed the twenty out of his hand and handed back his change. Cedric moved to the side and waited on his order.

"Jocelyn's friends stopped putting up missing posters, and they're meeting up for a gathering later," Alyssa mentioned.

"Are you going?" Carolyn checked.

"Not sure. I have to catch up on my studies," Alyssa replied.

"Order for mega combo," one of the staff called out.

Cedric heard his order being called. He grabbed the bag and drink, headed out of the burger place and back to his car. He snapped his fingers and remembered a load of laundry still needed to be folded, and planned to call the cable company to recheck his internet service. Cedric zoomed back to his place and strolled up, let himself in and sipped on his drink. For the past two weeks Professor Kenny Williams had given him the chance to lead discussions and he wanted to cram up on studies to be ready for the next quiz before testing happened. It was his last year as TA and he hoped to graduate with honors.

Right as Cedric dropped the bag on the table and unbuttoned his shirt, the doorbell rang. He groaned, turned and stomped back to the door, swiftly yanking it open.

"Cedric Washington?"

"Yes, who are you?"

"I'm Jessica Smith, a reporter-"

Cedric started to close the door on her but Jessica stuck her right foot in the door to block him.

"Mr. Washington, I have a few questions about Jocelyn Gambit, your former girlfriend," Jessica blurted out.

Cedric yanked the door open with his brows narrowed. "I've never dated Jocelyn."

"According to my notes, you've been seen around campus with Jocelyn, and at a few places off campus as well."

He held arms crossed. "I don't care what your notes say."

Jessica bit her bottom lip and held onto her pen with her pad open to take details down. She raked a hand through her hair. "So you two had a fling?"

Cedric stepped out of the entryway and clasped his hands together. "Jocelyn is a former student of Professor Williams. A few times I offered to help her study."

She cocked her head to the side. "Have you talked to Jocelyn lately?"

He started to close the door. "No, and I'd like for you to leave."

She stuck her hand out to block him.

"How long have you worked as a TA for Professor Kenny Williams?" Jessica continued her questions.

"None of your business. You're not a cop, so I don't

have to answer anything you ask." Cedric slammed the door in Jessica's face. He balled up his fist, leaned against it and closed his eyes. He counted to ten to relax and ease the pent-up anxiety that brewed up from his surprise visitor. Cedric hated for things to knock him off his square and lose control, he tried his best to stay out of the fray with most of the people in his neighborhood and campus life. On any given day, it could be something as simple as people coming in late to class, or the postman leaving his mail in the wrong placement, and a neighbor trying to. They all brought memories of growing up with strict parents that kept him on a tight leash. Trying out for activities meant more money out of their pockets, so he had to avoid arguments. Cedric worked hard and kept his head down, so he could make it on his own after graduation. He pulled the curtain in the front living room back and watched Jessica gaze back at the house. She'd researched and found he'd inherited the home from his parents after their deaths. Once she drove off, Cedric slouched down on the couch, grabbed his laptop and typed in Jocelyn's name to find out any more details.

"Jessica Smith, lead reporter on the murder of Jocelyn Gambit," Cedric mumbled to himself.

Reading details of her funeral being attended by fellow students, Cedric figured it would only be right if he showed up to give his prayers and thoughts at the meetup tonight on campus.

"Jessica Smith."

As soon as Cedric cleaned up and finished the rest of his workload, he drove back over to campus before it got too late. Normally on a Friday night, everyone was out partying at ten or eleven. Seeing the amount of people, not only students but faculty as well, impressed him the most, that people actually cared about each other in the world. He jogged up the stairs of the main building for Bengal College, which had been around for over thirty years. Nestled close to Times Square, with a famous basketball team and a few celebrities, Bengal became well-known as the college of many secrets. Cedric passed by a few students hugging and crying, some holding posters with Jocelyn's pictures on top. He slid up beside Alyssa and Carolyn talking with other students.

"Hey, we saw you earlier," Carolyn expressed.

Cedric smiled at her. "I had to come and give my regrets."

Alyssa frowned at his statement. "Your regards."

"Regrets," Cedric answered.

Alyssa and Carolyn both looked at each other and then hunched their shoulders. Cedric listened to the school's coach give a speech on being safe around campus and watching out for each other. Cedric's eyes peered at the canvas of people held up in groups, when he landed on Jessica Smith again.

Alyssa nudged him on the shoulder. "Hey, do you want one?"

He locked his eyes toward the piece of paper. "What?"

"A picture collage of Jocelyn. They're passing it around," Alyssa explained, holding up the one-page collage with Jocelyn's life on campus displayed.

"Sure, thanks." Cedric pursed his lips, and glanced back in the area Jessica stood, which was occupied by new people in her place.

The slow hums of a few people singing and offering prayers for Jocelyn's family mixed together under the moon shining across campus. Cedric felt worried by the interference of outside support hounding students and teachers with questions about Jocelyn's personal life. Him being friendly could come off differently to people and to know he'd been spotted with her so many times would spark interest with the police. He folded the paper, turned and started for his car. He headed back home to prepare for another day of work. He hoped the family could put her to rest and move on with their lives.

* * *

Alyssa hugged Carolyn goodnight, stepped out of her car and waved bye. It had been an emotional evening. Listening to the stories about Jocelyn and remembering the fun times throughout the years on campus made her death harder to take. Carolyn spoke about meeting with a counselor, and Alyssa agreed maybe she would try and schedule something after finals week was done. Carolyn drove away from the apartment building, turned the music up in her car, and made her way back to the other side of campus to her dorm room.

Bonnie Loston stumbled out of the cafe with her book bag on her shoulder, upset after her longtime boyfriend, Harper, broke up with her earlier in the day. Drowning herself in schoolwork helped to ease some of the pain, but she felt overwhelmed and needed one of her favorite ice cream sundaes to fix her heartache. Bonnie wiped the falling tears away from her cheek and lifted her shoulder to stop her bag from falling as she walked down the block to catch the last bus back to school.

"I hate you so much, Harper," Bonnie muttered to herself.

The long dark road was lit by the single street sign as

the cafe lights turned off with the closing sign flipped. Bonnie stepped forward and dropped the books in her bag as she tried to catch up to the bus that drove up to the stop sign without waiting.

Bonnie threw her hands up in the air. "No! You have got to be kidding me."

As the bus disappeared down the road, Bonnie bent down to scoop up her books and removed her cell from her bag to see it was low on battery life.

"What a night," Bonnie whispered, stood up and continued to walk down the street. After a few blocks and no one was around, Bonnie decided to try and call her ex to get a ride.

Bonnie held the phone up, dialed his number and listened to it ring back to back. "Come on, pick up," Bonnie murmured.

As she continued down the sidewalk a car pulled up alongside her that looked familiar.

Bonnie ended the call and rushed around to the passenger side. The doors unlocked and she climbed inside feeling hopeful. "Harper. I was just calling you." She dropped her smile when the gentleman grinned back at her.

"Oh my god. I thought you were my boyfriend."

A broad shoulder, muscular build, oval face with smooth skin, full lips, and dark eyes of the handsome man stared back at her and turned the music down in his car. "Sorry to disappoint."

Bonnie chortled, tossed her phone in her bag. "Oh no, I mean ex-boyfriend."

"Do you need a ride?"

"Uhm, I usually don't jump into cars. Are you sure?"

He motioned in the backseat at the groceries. "Positively. Had to pick up some groceries before heading home. Besides I have seen you around."

Bonnie glanced over her shoulder and swiftly he raised a needle in his hand and stuck her in the neck.

"What did yo-" Bonnie mumbled to herself, as her eyes grew heavy and darkness crept in around her.

He gently removed her book bag from her shoulder, along with her purse and threw them in the backseat. Then he moved Bonnie to lie back with her head on the window as he pressed two fingers on the side of her neck to check for her pulse that beat steady. He smiled and placed the car in drive and decided to enjoy his next present for a little while longer than he did Jocelyn.

The car drove off into the middle of the night. He glanced through the mirror as another car filled with young college boys yelling out of the window with alcohol bottles in their hands pulled up behind him.

"Get off the road!" one of them shouted, then flicked him off.

He shook his head. "Never be too careful at night."

Chapter Three

Jessica gripped her coat tighter around herself, shielding her body from the cold breeze in the early seven am morning. As she strode down the block from her morning coffee shop on her way to work, a lot was on her mind. She worried if she had pushed too hard questioning Cedric on campus about Jocelyn. As she approached the light to wait before crossing, she took a sip of her latte when a loud horn startled her and caused her almost to spill the drink. Jessica whipped her head around and saw Leo's hand up in the air. He put the car in park, hopped out and jogged around to talk to her.

Jessica glanced around the street at all the upset motorists because he was blocking the street.

"Leo, are you crazy?" she yelled.

Leo slipped a hand in his pocket and pulled out his phone. "I need to talk to you."

Jessica's eyes widened in shock, then she blew on her hands. "Well, this is not the way."

Leo held his phone out for Jessica to see the headline posted on the front page.

"*Missing college student Bonnie Loston.*" Jessica read the description, head tilted up to Leo's eyeline.

He nodded. "Another student, Jessica."

Jessica rubbed her forehead. "When did this happen?"

"Yesterday, last night."

"What are the police saying?"

Leo peered around the street, seeing the traffic picking up. "The second case dropped on my lap. Come with me so we can talk privately."

"I need to get going."

Leo walked off and opened the door for her to slide into the passenger side. "You can do that after we talk." Leo waved his hand toward the car.

Jessica stepped off the curb and hopped inside. "Where are we going?"

"To campus."

Jessica sighed and sat back, pulled on her seatbelt and prayed for Bonnie's safety. Leo pushed his hand out of the window to signal he was making a turn and sped through traffic down the road.

Jessica gulped down the rest of her drink. "Have you interviewed her family?"

"Not yet. I was still following up on Jocelyn's case when I got the call about Bonnie." Leo waited to pass a bus from West Avenue.

"Do you think it could be the same person?"

"Your guess is as good as mine."

Jessica gulped down the rest of her drink. "What does the captain say?"

"He says to treat it as an individual case, but I feel it in my bones. They're connected."

Jessica pointed at the folder on top of the dashboard. "Is this the folder on her?"

Leo reached over and passed the file to Jessica. "Yeah. We can remove any physical traits, because the girls look nothing alike, so he doesn't have a preference."

Jessica narrowed her eyes on the college schedule. "She's studying biology and has a boyfriend, Harper, the star of the basketball team."

"We can talk to him first."

Jessica sighed and closed the folder. "Very weird. Right as Jocelyn is found, another girl is taken."

"I want him caught," Leo demanded, as he swerved in and out traffic. He stopped at the light a block from the campus.

Jessica glanced out of the window to the front entrance, noticing Cedric laughing with a student as they walked into the building.

"Have you talked with any of the professors or TAs?" Jessica questioned. The news of another young woman being taken seemed to leave Leo defeated and frustrated at the same time.

Leo hooked his hand around the knob of the door to swing it open and allowed Jessica to stroll in first. He gently touched her on the shoulder to head toward the sign for the administration office on the right.

"A few follow up discussions about Jocelyn."

Jessica scanned the halls of Bengal College taking deep breaths, playing the old memories in her mind. What if she'd done more to really advocate for women on campus or try and spread the word when she became a journalist? Maybe some of the tragedies wouldn't have happened. They came upon the front office and waited for the secretary to finish her call.

"Hello, I need to speak with the president of the college, Mr. Dean Chancellor."

She hung up the phone and stood. "And you are?"

Leo removed his badge and held up to her face. "Detective Leo Walsh and this is reporter Jessica Smith. We're here about another disappearance. Bonnie Guston."

"Oh, yes, poor thing. Please come inside. Dean is waiting for you." The secretary came from behind her desk and ushered them down the corridor to his office. She knocked and gently opened the door as President Chancellor wrapped up a call and waved for them to enter.

"President Dean Chancellor," Leo announced.

"Please, call me Dean."

Leo pointed over his shoulder. "Detective Walsh and this is Jessica."

President Chancellor raised his hand and Jessica extended hers for a shake and took a seat.

"Thank you both for coming so quickly." President Chancellor exhaled and sat down in his chair.

Leo removed a notepad and pen from his shirt pocket. "Tell us what you know so far."

"Well, not much really. My assistants went to her dorm room and nothing was out of place." President Chancellor sat forward and clasped his hands together.

"How long has she been a student?" Leo questioned.

"About two years," President Chancellor explained.

"Does she have any friends, maybe a boyfriend?" Jessica inquired.

Dean paused briefly and stared at her. "I honestly have no clue. You seem familiar."

Leo and Jessica glanced at each other. "She's a reporter."

President Chancellor snapped his fingers. "That's where I know your face. Is this going to be on television?" President Chancellor asked.

Jessica and Leo were surprised by his question. "Uhm, I think for now we will keep the details to ourselves," Leo responded.

"Of course, I just think having television news talk with me would bring a lot of notice to Bengal College and bring awareness," President Chancellor answered.

Leo folded his notebook closed and stared at Dean Chancellor. His antenna went up. People like Chancellor were fame hungry and any type of recognition to be in the spotlight would propel his career, regardless of a young woman being missing or possibly dead.

"Mr. Chancellor, can you tell us how Bonnie's grades are looking?"

"Her grades, yes. Let me check the system." President Chancellor entered the campus database a few seconds later and turned the monitor around to face Jessica and Leo.

Leo rubbed his chin. "So she's on top of her grades. No problems there."

"Does she work at all or have a campus internship?" Jessica checked.

President Chancellor wrote on a piece of paper. "She's not on any financial scholarship from what I see. I think maybe talking to her professors will help. Here's Professor Williams' room number down the hall to the right."

Leo picked it up and Jessica rose from the chair, then followed him out of the office.

"That was interesting," Jessica mentioned, as she removed the piece of paper out of his hand.

"He's looking to be famous," Leo grumbled. He marched down the hall to Professor Williams' door and knocked.

A few seconds went by and it opened to Cedric holding a clipboard in his hand.

Jessica dropped her smile and took stock of the set of his mouth trying to hide a frown. "Hello, is Professor Williams here?"

"He is. Let me get him for you," Cedric replied and glanced toward Professor Williams as he wrote on the board.

Jessica took in the appearance of the older gentleman with gray hair and broad shoulders. He glanced at Cedric talking to the two people interrupting his class session. Professor Williams approached the door. Cedric left to continue directing the class on the agenda for the day.

Leo lifted his badge out of his pocket. "Professor Williams, I'm detective Leo Walsh."

Professor Williams removed his glasses. "Yes, what's this about?"

"About one of your students Bonnie Loston."

"Bonnie, what happened?"

"She's missing, sir. Has no one explained about her disappearance?" Leo queried.

Professor Williams stated, "No. My workload has me slammed back to back with classes and work projects outside of the classroom."

"What kind of work projects?" Jessica wondered.

"A few students who want extra credit. I help them take on projects in real life situations."

"Like an internship?"

"Paid study. They follow and interview someone who matches their goals in life," Professor William informed them, while holding his book to his chest.

Jessica took in Professor Williams' demeanor and he seemed more concerned for Bonnie and more open to help with information on her disappearance than President Chancellor. She remembered her time on campus a few years ago when professors only cared about getting to the next task and less about connecting with the students.

Leo read off on his notes. "We know Bonnie has good grades. Can you tell us if she had a job in your program or anything about her relationship with her boyfriend? I believe his name is Harper."

Professor Williams cupped his chin. "I heard her arguing one time with someone outside the classroom, but it was a while ago."

"Do you remember the person's name?"

Professor Williams gestured to his classroom. "I don't, but Cedric broke up the conversation. He might know," Professor Williams explained.

"Was Jocelyn Gambit a student of yours at some point?" Jessica blurted out.

Professor Williams cleared his throat. "Possibly. I see a lot of students throughout the years."

"We'd love to get the name or description from Cedric," Leo replied.

"Sure, let me grab him." Professor Williams stepped back in his classroom and waved for Cedric to come to the door.

"Yes, Professor Williams," Cedric said, standing in the entryway.

"Bonnie Loston is missing. Do you remember the guy she was arguing with a few months ago outside the classroom?" Professor Williams asked.

Cedric looked from Leo to Jessica and back at the professor. "I never got a name, sorry. It was so fast and she rushed inside upset."

"Do you remember how he looked?" Jessica checked.

"Tall, dark hair, slender build maybe."

"Kind of like you," Jessica observed and all eyes cascaded down on her.

Leo pressed a hand on her shoulder and smiled. "Professor, thank you for your time. I will be in touch." Professor Williams nodded and Cedric's glare faded as Leo gently nudged Jessica to start walking away.

"What was that?"

"He's hiding something."

"Jessica, you can't start that again."

"Start what?"

"Accusing people of vibes."

Jessica stopped walking and threw a hand on her hip. "My vibes helped you solve a lot of cases, if I recall."

Leo shook his head. "Yeah, and almost got me fired."

"Let's go to Bonnie's dorm room and see if anything points to her boyfriend." Jessica ignored his comment.

Leo pointed at a group of girls walking and laughing together across campus in the same direction to the dorm rooms. "Hey, isn't that Jocelyn's friends, Carolyn and Alyssa?"

"They might know Bonnie, too."

Leo jogged toward the group as they approached the door. "Come on, let's catch up."

"Excuse me, ladies," Jessica announced, making their heads whip around in her direction.

"Yes?" Carolyn answered.

"Aren't you Jocelyn's friends?" Leo probed.

Alyssa rubbed a hand up and down her arm nervously. "We are." She gulped through a dry throat.

Jessica held a hardened brow. "I saw you at the gathering here the other day in her honor."

Leo stuck his badge up in the air. "I wanted to ask if you knew Bonnie Loston."

"Bonnie." Alyssa gasped and grasped Carolyn's hand.

"She's missing."

Both of them gasped in shock.

Alyssa placed a hand over her mouth as tears pooled in her eyes. "First, Jocelyn and now, Bonnie."

Carolyn stumbled backwards. Her eyes rolled to the back of her head and she fainted.

"Oh my god!" Alyssa shouted, scrambling to grab Carolyn as she tumbled to the ground.

Jessica and Leo dragged her inside the building to a couch and Alyssa rushed to grab a cup of water as another student yelled for medical attention. Jessica had it in her mind this would be a quick conversation, but it had become way bigger than she ever anticipated. Leo removed the cup of water from Alyssa and bent down to press it to Carolyn's lips.

Alyssa waved at the nurse as she ran through the corridor. "Over here! She fainted." Jessica slipped her phone out of her pocket.

Ellen: *How are things going?*

Jesscia: *One of the girls that knows Joceyln fainted. We can talk later.*

Ellen: *Keep me updated.*

Jessica made a note to follow up with her editor to find another person to handle this story because it was becoming a bigger situation than it initially was presented to her that day.

Jessica wiped the sweat from her forehead. "This is too much."

Chapter Four

A few items on his shopping list shouldn't have taken this long to grab, but he came during the late afternoon. He brushed past the large crowds hovered in the middle of the aisle at the grocery store. Dinner needed to be on time like always or his mood would shatter and cause undo tension for other people. Like always, he needed to get back to his home and set up his dinner date and show off the gifts he'd bought her. Being the best boyfriend was his goal and he liked to impress them before he had to hurt anyone. Women were complicated from what he knew and liked to be impressed, spoiled, and nurtured, so he wanted to pick up some roses and chocolates as a special occasion.

"Did you hear about that missing girl at the college up the street?"A woman in line spoke to another girl standing behind him.

Another customer popped her gum in her mouth, picking up a magazine. "They need to shut that place down. I heard so many stories."

"I'll be glad when they find the prick."

He smirked, removed the items from his basket and placed them on the conveyor belt.

After paying, he walked to his car and dropped the groceries in the backseat and paused when someone tapped on his window.

"Excuse me you dropped this, sir." The same woman behind him held his wallet in her hand.

"Thank you. I didn't notice it was missing."

She smiled and glanced to his backseat and noticed the garden tools on the seat. "Doing some late night gardening?"

He frowned.

She pointed and chuckled at his backseat. "The tools."

He laughed and shrugged. "Green thumb."

She shook her head and gave him a small wave. "Have a nice night."

"You as well." He watched her walk over to her car and talk with the other young woman and they motioned to him.

He winked and she blushed.

Soon as he pulled off into traffic he thought about how close he came to being spread across the news and social media. The anticipation of the police digging into his background and posting some of his desirable choices in what he likes to do to women, because in his mind they should be grateful for the attention. It wasn't his fault. Too many of the women needed someone to guide them and love them properly, but got distracted by how society wanted them to be with the rich and famous man. He turned onto his street and parked in his garage, gathered his things and strode in the house to the tv playing. He kicked off his shoes, took off his coat and put down his groceries. He jogged upstairs to hop in the shower. Dinner that night was steak, vegetables, and chocolates, with a little dancing if she acted right. Once he changed his clothes he came downstairs and unpacked the food and put everything out to prepare. After tossing the trash away, he trekked over to the basement door, removed the lock and turned the light on. He went down the stairs to see his favorite girl asleep, wearing his favorite color blue.

"Wake up, sleepyhead."

Bonnie slowly flicked her eyes open. She felt sluggish, like she'd been sleeping for days.

She mumbled under her breath, eyes watery as he caressed her cheek.

"Shush, now. Be a good girl."

Bonnie shook her head, squirming to get out of the tight ropes. Her eyes dashed around the lit small room.

He clipped her chin. "If I take this off, will you be quiet?"

Bonnie nodded.

He slowly pulled the duct tape from her mouth. "There you go."

"Please let me go," she begged. Tears fell down her cheeks as she thought about her family and friends.

A sigh escaped his lips. "I thought you wanted to be here."

Bonnie whimpered. "I want to go home."

"Jocelyn said the same thing at first, but over time she loved me."

"Please let me go."

He stood up and gripped her by the arm to sit her up. "I have dinner ready for us and your favorite chocolates."

Bonnie jerked out of his hold and stumbled to the ground in front of him and he chuckled.

"Bonnie, your legs and hands are tied up. You aren't leaving me."

He remembered Jocelyn once fought him and lost. She ended up buried before he could have his time with her. He'd hate to do the same to Bonnie. He reached down and lifted her up bridal style and carried her upstairs.

"We will have dinner together and dance, with a little champagne."

"Help me! Somebody help!" Bonnie screamed, jerking in his hold.

He covered her mouth once he got upstairs and placed her on the couch. He turned up the jazz music to drown out the sounds.

"No one can hear you, baby."

Bonnie's wrinkled brow canvassed the living room. "My boyfriend is looking for me. He's going to kill you."

He laughed and stood straight up, knowing they'd broken up that night. He'd heard the entire conversation.

"Funny he never picked you up from the diner."

Bonnie froze at his comment, eyes scanned up his frame. "How many women have you kidnapped?"

He tapped her on the nose. "Stop worrying and have dinner with me."

"Are you going to kill me?"

"Do you want red or white wine?"

"I want to go home."

"Red wine is the best."

Bonnie tracked the distance from the door to the kitchen, then of how long it would take to remove the ropes from her feet and hands. Her parents explained to always go with a group of people instead of alone at night, but she felt she could handle herself. Well, that night proved she should have listened because her life hadn't been the same for the past few days. Luckily he hadn't tried to touch her, but tonight seemed like another story.

"Here, drink this."

Bonnie jerked her head back and pushed the cup away. "I don't drink."

He frowned and cupped her chin to widen her mouth. "Drink it, Bonnie."

She grabbed the glass from him and lifted it to her lips and smelled the strong odor. Something smelt funny.

"It's strong."

He plopped down on the couch, clapped a hand on her thigh. "You will love it. Come on, tell me about yourself."

"How long do you plan on keeping me here?"

"I met you for the first time at Bengal College."

She paused at his words. "You've been stalking me. I thought you were a nice person."

He grinned. "Is that what you call people that meet each other in person and become friends?"

"I think you've made a terrible mistake. It's not too late."

He gulped down the red wine. "Drink up. Dinner is ready."

Bonnie tossed the drink in his face and bashed him over the head with the glass. She hopped up and tried to get to the door as he slowly tried to stand and gather a towel to clean his face from the gash on the side of his head.

"Bitch!"

Bonnie took a hop to the door and yanked on the knob, screaming and banging for help.

"Help me!"

"Nobody can hear you, Bonnie."

She searched for any type of weapon and found a book on the table and tossed it at his head, but he ducked before it landed.

"Since you want to play games, it's time you went back to the basement."

Bonnie shook her head and headbutted him, which dazed her in the process and she fell down on the floor as they both withered in pain.

The next morning he pulled himself up off the floor and smoothed his palm around the back of his neck and side of his face. It was tender to the touch, and a little swollen as he rose from the couch. He'd locked Bonnie back up in the basement, finished dinner by himself and showered before falling asleep on the couch to an old black and white movie.

"She's just like the rest," he grumbled. He moved around the bathroom and brushed his teeth. Right then he made up his mind to get rid of her and find someone else to love him and share his home as a real couple.

He stalked out of the bathroom to the blaring of the tv screen with the latest broadcast on Bengal College.

"We have the latest details of Bonnie Loston as the victim of a kidnapping. Jessica Smith, one of New York Gazette's finest journalists, is here with us today. Jessica, what can you tell us about her or her family?"

"Thank you for having me. Unfortunately the police are in the early stages, so I can't give out any major details, beyond what is known of her last whereabouts at a local diner," Jessica expressed.

After hearing the newscast, he strode over to the door for the basement. He opened the door, pressed on the light and marched down the stairs. Bonnie was laid out on the cot under a blanket. He had her tied up again.

He pushed a piece of her hair back and whispered, "We could have been good together, Bonnie."

The doorbell ringing pulled him away from his next movements as Bonnie started to wake up.

"Where am I?" she remarked, slowly opening her eyes remembering back to last night.

Ding!

He covered her mouth and glared. "Keep quiet or you die."

Bonnie's eyes blinked back twice and he removed his hand.

"Good girl."

He sprinted up the stairs, shut the lights off and locked it behind him, then ran to answer the door.

"Hi, we're selling cookies for our school." A group of young girls with their mother held up signs.

"I love cookies! Please come inside and let me grab my wallet."

The excitement in their eyes made him feel accomplished and he took the form from their hands and filled out the paperwork. He grabbed his wallet and took out one hundred dollars.

"Thank you!"

"You are welcome."

"Wow! This is such a thoughtful gift. We've knocked on so many doors. You're the first to actually answer," one of the girls' mother said.

"A lot of older people in the neighborhood so that's probably why you don't get much activity."

The little blond girl with braces pointed to the broken glass on the floor near the couch. "What's that?"

He swirled his head around to check and flashed a wide smile. "I broke a glass last night. I thought I got everything cleaned up. Silly me."

The mom of the group huddled them up close. "Be careful and don't cut your feet, girls."

"Here you go, mister. Cookies will come in two weeks." The older girl with long braids handed him a receipt.

"Have a good day, sir." All the girls waved goodbye.

He dropped the smile after shutting the door to stare at the mess he missed last night.

"I wanted her to be special."

Every woman he'd taken at one point was special in his mind and he claimed to want to make it last, but they'd all fought him and became a burden to the point that killing them became a great satisfaction.

Chapter Five

Jessica lifted her pen from her bag and stuck it in between the pages of Bonnie's chemistry book toward the last page Bonnie was reading. She sighed, pulled the pen away and moved it over the desk to the other documents laid out from the last time Bonnie was in her dorm room. Her day started out checking in on Carolyn to get an update on if she was back home after fainting. Alyssa said she was sleeping and then promised to run by later today if she felt up to company. Jessica moved around the room noticing Bonnie's bed still not made from the week of her disappearance, her clothes scattered around. Lately the school had tried to do group meetups when going and coming from campus. Jessica wanted to interview a few more people before following up with Leo on any new updates. Bonnie still had a chance to be found, and Jessica hoped whoever took her knew they'd be caught soon.

"Talk to me, Bonnie. Where are you?" Jessica muttered to herself, lifting the picture of Bonnie with her boyfriend.

"He hasn't said anything since she was taken. Why is that?"

Jessica placed the picture back in its place, bent down and scanned the calendar over her whiteboard.

Jessica reached in her pocket to grab her phone. "Dinner with boobear at our regular spot." She turned and walked out of the dorm room and bumped into a surprised visitor.

"Shit! Who are you?"

Jessica furrowed her right brow. "Who are you?" She glanced at her phone connecting with Leo and hung up.

"I came to get my things from Bonnie."

"Bonnie's your girlfriend right?"

Harper avoided eye contact and exhaled a breath. "We broke up."

"Right, I forgot. Can you tell me what your last conversation was like?"

"Ugh. Pretty much I told her I wanted to break up, needed space."

"You and Bonnie dated for a year and she was okay with the breakup?"

Harper flung his gym bag over his shoulder. "Hold up, who are you again?"

"I never said."

"Then I don't have to answer your questions." He moved around her and headed into the room. He located his basketball shoes and book bag in the corner of the room. The tall, lanky built athlete grumbled under his breath and propped open Bonnie's top drawer, taking the few shirts he left in her room. Jessica crossed her arms over her chest and monitored his movements.

"I'm working with the police to find Bonnie."

He paused at her statement. "Is she still alive? I mean,

I know when people go missing the first twenty-four hours are the most important."

"I noticed you two went to have dinner the night of her going missing."

Harper frowned and dropped his bag on the floor. "What are you asking me?"

Jessica shrugged, pushed off the wall and stepped over to the calendar on the wall. She pointed her finger at the date. "Dinner at your usual spot."

He exhaled a breath and raked a hand through his hair. "We often went to the cafe at least once a week to hang out. Look, Bonnie wanted more than I was able to give."

"Well, being in a relationship that tends to happen."

"I'm still young. I never wanted to be tied down."

"So you got rid of her," Jessica argued.

Harper breathed slowly. His eyes raised high, and he waved his hands left to right. "What! No way. I have nothing to do with Bonnie going missing."

"The police think it's someone she knew."

Harper pointed to his chest. "The only thing I'm guilty of is leaving her at the cafe and I explained it to the police and her family."

"And Jocelyn?"

"Never spoken to Jocelyn."

"That's funny because a few people have seen you two together around campus."

He bent down to grab up his bag. He threw it across his shoulder. "I'm one of the star athletes. Come on, man."

"I guess being the star athlete comes in handy."

He paused at the door, holding it wide open. "What is that supposed to mean?"

"Often the star boyfriend gets away with the crime."

Jessica strode out of the entryway and bumped him in the shoulder. Hearing the ringing of her phone she lifted it up and cursed, remembering she'd called Leo earlier.

"Hey."

Leo fussed. "You called me and then hung up."

"Sorry, I got distracted for a second." Jessica stopped in the hall before stepping on the elevator after noticing President Chancellor on a phone call that looked heated. His hands flew in the air before he hung up and climbed on the elevator.

"Where are you?"

"In Bengal, checking out Bonnie's dorm room."

"Find anything new?"

"Not really, but I did meet her boyfriend."

"He bring you any fresh information?"

Jessica ran and jumped on the elevator and prayed she caught up with him. "I'm on the elevator. It might cut off."

"Why are you talking low?"

"No reason."

The elevator came to a stop. Jessica moved through the crowd and gazed at Mr. Chancellor talking with another student holding a bag of laundry in her hands.

"Let me call you back."

"Wait, Jess-"

Jessica disconnected, tucking the cell back in her pocket she eased in closer to their conversation.

"I have put in two complaints about my roommate," she complained, and hoisted the laundry in her hands.

President Chancellor rubbed her arm up and down, then started to walk around to leave through the exits.

"Liddy, calm down and talk with your resident assistant. I don't have time right now."

Liddy stomped her foot. "But it's not fair."

President Chancellor rolled his eyes and gestured with his hands to lower her voice. "Control yourself, Liddy. We've talked about your attitude."

Liddy straightened up, scanned the lounge area of the dorms and nodded.

Dean Chancellor smiled, then pat her on the shoulder. "Talk to the RA and then we'll talk later."

Liddy poked her lip out and stormed down the hall and Jessica continued to follow Mr. Chancellor out of the building, moving slowly through the crowd of people coming in and out and headed toward the parking lot.

Jessica dropped low behind a white jeep when Dean swiftly glanced over his shoulder, then hopped in his black Hyundai two cars away.

"What are you up to, Chancellor?" Jessica whispered and watched him start his car and pull out of the reserved parking space. Her gut was saying to call Leo, but it would take him forever to catch up. So she hopped in her car, snapped a picture of Chancellor's license plate, backed out of the parking space and stayed two cars behind him. They turned at the stop sign, swerving into traffic. Jessica turned on her Bluetooth and dialed Leo's phone number.

"I can't talk right now, Jess."

"Run this license plate."

"Should I be worried?" Leo groaned.

"Probably. Dean Chancellor left campus. I'm right behind him going down Sixth Street."

"Jessica, stay back and don't get involved."

Jessica rolles her eyes. "I promise."

"Based on your past, I doubt you're going to stay put."

Jessica scanned the street signs. "He's stopped at the light. Looks like we're heading toward Times Square."

"Shit. Alright, be careful."

Jessica rushed forward. "I will."

"Jessica, do you hear me?"

Their call disconnected and Jessica hung up and parked a block from Chancellor. She rushed to remove her seatbelt, climbed out of the car and jogged to catch up to Dean going into the park. She looked behind her back, bit her lip and edged in close. Jessica watched him hold out his arms and hug someone she couldn't make out in the distance. Dean once again peeked over his shoulder and Jessica stumbled to fall behind the tree to not be noticed. She caught the tail end of Dean wrapping an arm around their shoulder and squeezing but a crowd of bikers rode through her path cutting off her view.

Jessica jumped up and down to get a better close up look. "Fuck!"

Almost each biker raised their hand in excitement causing Jessica to miss Dean leave from where he was standing. She glanced from left to right, and no one matched his description or the person he met.

Jessica raked a hand through her hair, blew out a breath and sprinted back to the parking lot. When she made it back to the lot, Chancellor's car was gone.

"Who are you really, Mr. Chancellor?" Jessica mumbled to herself.

* * *

Jessica carried her groceries in her arms down the street, exhausted from a long day of investigating. All she could think about was a hot shower and beef fried rice and vegetables. Jessica smiled to one of the delivery people who often came by her office. As she moved to the stoplight, she dropped her smile seeing Cedric laughing as he came out of a bar with a young lady who she recalled President Chancellor talking with earlier. The walk sign changed to go and she headed forward and kept her eyes ahead and waited to see if he'd remember her.

"Hey, Cedric."

Cedric and Liddy paused. "Uhm, hey. Do I know you?"

"Not personally, but it's nice seeing you again outside of the police questioning."

Liddy's eyes ballooned at her comment about the police. "Police? Is something wrong, Cedric?"

Cedric chuckled and grasped Liddy's hand. "I helped the police about Jocelyn."

"Liddy, right? Sorry to interrupt your date. I just saw Cedric and wanted to let him know we've got a few leads on Bonnie's disappearance."

Cedric glared at her words. "We have to go."

"Hey, thanks again!" Jessica yelled.

"Cedric, what is she talking about in your relationship?" Liddy argued and Cedric waved his hands in the air.

Jessica watched them for a brief moment going back and forth. She strode into her building, gestured at the security staff then walked on the elevator as a woman held it open when she came off.

Jessica unlocked the door to her apartment and stepped inside. She flipped on the lights and let her jacket and purse slip from her shoulders. She toed out of her shoes and lowered to the floor when her cat came into the living room. Jessica smiled, caressed the top of her head and marched to the kitchen. She grabbed her groceries and put the bread, cheese, and meat away. Jessica turned on the stove and tossed her apron on and started to cook her dinner.

"You miss me today, sweetie?"

Her cat drank from her water bowl and Jessica poured a glass of wine and stood with her back to the stove.

"Cedric, Dean Chancellor, something is weird about you two." Jessica paced in her kitchen talking to herself, then gulped down the rest of her wine. She trekked into the living room, picked up her bag and removed all of the information on the case. She plopped down on the couch, stuffed her feet underneath her legs and started reading over the details of Jocelyn.

Chapter Six

That same night, Leo handed a single rose to his date and smiled in her face. For the longest time, Chelsie, one of the paralegals at a local law firm, had her eye on Leo. Every other day she'd bring him lunch or call to check on his day. At first Leo wanted nothing to do with Chelsie because of their jobs, but eventually he got to know her and found her to have a nice personality and was selfless. It didn't hurt that Chelsie was at least five-seven, with long curly hair, full lips, curves, and long legs. Leo lifted the wine menu and suggested what Chelsie would want for the evening.

"Do you like Roses?"

Chelsie placed her hand on top of his hand, rubbed across his knuckles. "Anything is fine with me."

The waitress approached their table and logged into her device to take their orders.

"Can we get white wine and caviar to start out."

"Coming right up." Their waitress filled their glasses with water.

Color rose high on Chelsie's cheeks. "So, I finally got you on a date."

Leo smirked, then grabbed his glass of water to take a sip. "You act like I turned you down because I didn't like you."

"Felt like that, Mr. Walsh."

"Come on, you know every guy at the precinct wants you."

Chelsie seductively caressed a hand up his arm. "I only have eyes for one person."

Leo winked his left eye and flipped the dinner menu open. "What are we having?"

"Whatever you want."

Leo closed the menu and stared at her. "Chelsie what's going on?"

"What do you mean?"

"Are you going to agree with everything I say tonight?"

"No."

"Okay, so what do you want for dinner?"

Chelsie clasped her hands together and leaned forward on the table. "I will take the lobster and pasta."

Leo closed the menu and handed it off to the waitress. "That sounds good."

The server came back to the table with the bottle of wine and laid out the caviar. The server filled each wine glass and handed each one a napkin.

"Are we ready to order?" she asked.

"We'll both have the stuffed lobster and pasta with cream sauce on top," Leo ordered, picking up his glass of white wine.

Their server typed in the order and smiled. "Coming right up.

Chelsie spread a small amount of caviar on her bread and lifted it to Leo's mouth. "Try this and tell me it's not good."

Leo opened his mouth and ate from her finger and smiled. "Not bad."

"You know caviar can be an aphrodisiac."

He chuckled and took another piece of the entree.

"So tell me about yourself. How long have you been single?"

"Single for two years, dating on and off for the last six months," Cheslie offered.

Right as Leo opened his mouth to reply, his phone interrupted. Leo raised his finger to pause for a moment.

"Walsh."

The waitress arrived with their dinner and handed Chelsie her meal, and placed Leo's plate on the table.

"Right now? Can't you-"

Chelsie's face caved into a frown at his conversation.

"Okay, I will be there. Alright! I got it," Leo groaned, and clicked the end button.

Chelsie sat back in her seat and glowered at him. "You're leaving."

Leo laid his napkin on the table and exhaled a breath. He reached in his pants pocket for his wallet and removed cash to pay for the dinner.

"I wish I could stay, but work called."

"Work or another woman?"

"What are you talking about, Chelsie?"

"Jessica Smith."

Leo's head bucked back in confusion. "Jessica?"

Cheslie nodded. "I see her always around you at the station. What else am I supposed to think?"

"Jessica and I are friends, but we work together."

"So you've never wanted to date her or have sex with her?" Chelsie challenged.

Leo bent down and kissed Chelsie on the cheek and cupped her chin. "I will call you when I get a free moment."

"Promise me something."

"Chelsie."

"You'll give us a chance."

"I will call you."

* * *

Thirty minutes later Leo parked at an abandoned building on the outskirts of Brooklyn. He stepped from his vehicle and held up his badge to the local officer.

"What am I doing here, Mark?" Leo asked, as they trekked inside of the warehouse.

Mark bent down and pulled the sheet back. "I thought you might want to know Jocelyn's body was found."

Leo ran a hand down his mouth. "Fuck."

"Yep, same thing I said. I know they had a funeral already, but at least you can give the family closure."

"What happened?"

"I got a call from an anonymous number about a van that was stopped off over here and the place has been shut down for a few years."

Leo motioned around the area. "Who all lives over here?"

"Mostly older couples. A few drug addicts pop up. It's not the best place to stay."

"Cause of death?"

"From the initial check, I saw marks around her neck, but we can't be too sure."

"I want the full report."

"You're still working the case."

"The captain wanted to close the case, but if we can make some connections to lead on Bonnie's disappearance, we could catch this guy."

Mark removed his gloves and stepped out of the warehouse to a barrage of reporters turning on their cameras.

Leo threw his hands up in the air. "Who called the fucking press?"

"They will turn everything into a shitshow."

"I need to go knock on some doors. Can you handle them?"

Mark slapped hands with Leo. "I got you, man."

A few reporters pushed through the crowd and shoved cameras in Leo's face. While blocking them with his hand, he thought he saw Chelsie's black Porsche sitting across the street.

"Is she following me?" Leo muttered under his breath and marched to the house two blocks from the warehouse. The lights on the Porsche came on and the car drove off in the opposite direction when he stepped on the porch, raised his hand, and knocked on the door.

"Hello, I'm-"

"We don't know anything," the older woman answered.

"Ma'am, I'm not here to arrest you."

The gray haired woman grumbled and started to slam the door in his face. "You're the police. Why should I trust you?"

"Please, we got an anonymous call from this address," Leo lied, trying to get her to open up.

She squinted her eyes and pulled the door back to allow him to step into her home. On the outside it looked worn down with busted stairs and crumbling bars on the windows. When you actually got into the home, it was decorated with warm colors. There was a full couch, a big screen tv hanging on the wall, pictures of family members, and a large table.

"I never called about next door."

"My name is Leo Walsh. I'm a detective investigating a rash of missing young women. How long have you lived here?"

"Thirty years. I'm Nell Wallen."

"Do you live alone, Nell?"

"Yeah, after my husband Gerald died, my son wanted me to move, but I told him this was our dream home."

"Can you tell me about your neighbors, Nell?"

"You want something to drink? Not much to tell. Gloria lives two doors down across the way with her grandson, and a few young couples live on the next block."

Leo shook his head no, then pulled his notepad from his jacket. "Gloria's grandson. What do you know about him?"

Nell limped toward the kitchen and pulled the fridge open to grab a Diet Coke. "He's in and out of jail all the time. The boy is just dumb."

Leo smirked.

"Are the girls they've talked about on the tv from that college?"

"Yes, ma'am."

"Mhmmm."

"Anything you can think of today? Like someone driving around that looked out of place?"

"I got home an hour ago. My bingo was tonight."

Leo smiled and closed his booklet and started to leave.

Nell took a seat in her recliner and kicked her feet up. "I do remember a few nights ago maybe, a car was parked for a few minutes out front of the building, but they left when I came outside to take out my trash."

"Thank you, Mrs. Wallen. You've been very helpful."

"Detective Walsh."

Leo paused at the door. "Yes?"

"Nothing good comes from that building, especially at night."

"Hopefully we can get things cleared up soon and safe for everyone."

Nell chuckled and lifted her drink to take a sip. "They will never let that happen."

"Who are they?"

"Same people that put money in your pocket."

"Are you talking about bribery?"

Nell shrugged her shoulders. "Keep your eyes open, Detective Walsh."

Leo headed out of her home and jogged down the stairs back to his car. He stared at each home and back to the warehouse where Mark was still talking with reporters. "You too, Mrs. Wallen. You as well."

Ring!

A flash of Jessica's name made Leo hop in his car and answer quickly. "Before you say anything, I'm leaving a crime scene. Are you at home?"

"Yes. I think I found something."

"Me too."

"Be careful driving, Leo."

"What? You sound like you care about me." Leo laughed.

Jessica tittered and cleared her throat as the silence filled the phone.

Chapter Seven

Jessica stretched her arms out and yawned, pulled the covers back from off the couch and glanced around her living room. The smell of coffee caused her to jump up in panic thinking someone else was there when she forgot Leo was on his way.

He stepped out of the kitchen holding a cup for her in his right hand. She glanced at the clock on her table and saw midnight.

"I called you an hour ago."

"Sorry I had to go home and change first."

"You had a date, right?"

Leo slouched down in the love seat opposite of her. "Something like that."

Jessica grasped her blanket and laid it across her lap, lifted the files and notes from her investigation.

Jessica blew over her cup. "What happened? She ghosted you?" Jessica teased.

Leo stared at Jessica for a brief second, shook his head and put the coffee down on the table stand. "Nope, so what do you have for me?"

"Since you're keeping secrets, maybe I should keep mine."

"Jess, we both know you can't hold water."

Jessica stuck her tongue out at him. "Anyway, after going through all the files and notes on both girls, I checked the Bengal database with police records of students."

"We already looked into school."

"But you never looked into girls that are close to Jocelyn and Bonnie."

"What do you mean?"

"They're both friends with Alyssa and Carolyn. At first you could overlook it, but it drove me nuts."

Leo stood and joined Jessica on the couch as she passed him the booklet. "Okay. Keep talking."

Jessica jumped up and walked off.

"Where are you going?"

Jessica pulled the whiteboard she had in the corner up. "I need to grab my chart."

The entire board was filled with details on the case for both girls, from family information to eating habits.

"Jocelyn was taken close to a month ago, then Bonnie a few days later right."

"I follow so far."

"I think he got scared after we approached Carolyn and Alyssa. Bonnie's boyfriend has classes with Alyssa and Carolyn lives in the same dorm as Bonnie."

"Why these two girls?"

"I think they were supposed to be taken."

Leo's mouth fell agape.

"Yeah, I had the same expression."

"We found Jocelyn's body. Last night I got the call while on my date."

"Exactly, which tells me he's going to grab someone either today or tomorrow."

"So Bonnie's probably going to be killed soon."

"I spoke to her boyfriend at her dorm."

"Jessica, you know talking with him by yourself could have led you to getting arrested."

"He's not thinking about me. Besides, the way he's so full of himself, any woman with common sense will stay away."

She groaned and threw her hand up in exasperation. "I need to follow up with him."

"He's got a game coming up so we can head over to talk to him together."

Jessica handed Leo the chart board and walked off annoyance across her face.

"Where are you going?"

"To bed," she snapped.

Leo shook his head and blew out a breath. "So you're going to leave me to go through all these notes!"

"Have fun."

"Have fun," Leo said, mocking Jessica. He threw his head back on the couch and groaned.

Jessica shut her bedroom door, slid out of her house shoes and laid down in the bed and turned the light off.

* * *

A pillow came down on Leo's head. He frowned and glanced up at Jessica standing with her bag in her hand.

"Let's go."

Leo held his arm up to check the time on his watch. "What time is it?"

"Nine am. We need to hurry up and get to the college."

"First I gotta check in with the captain."

"Can't wait until later?"

"No, and I need to get home to change."

"You took a shower already."

"Jessica, be serious. It was after a date last night."

"Well, are you saying you two did something that would cause you to shower right afterwards?"

Leo threw the cover backwards and rose from the couch, stretching his arm wide. "Why are you so nosy about my love life?"

He noticed Jessica's eyes glued to his chest and waved his hand in front of her face.

"Huh."

"Where did you go just now?"

Jessica turned and marched toward the door. "Come on, you're holding up my day." Jessica ignored his statement.

Leo shook his head, put on his shoes and grunted. He snatched up his keys and phone and trailed behind Jessica out of her apartment.

It didn't take long to get on the road and soon the two of them pulled up to a stop sign. Leo tapped his fingers on the steering wheel as the music played on the radio. Gazing out of the rearview window, he noticed the same black Porsche from last night at the crime scene. Abruptly Leo made a U-turn, cut the car off and stopped traffic as cars honked their horns. Leo jumped out of the car and Jessica yelled his name.

"Leo, are you crazy!"

"Stay in the car!" Leo shouted, stomped over to the

car and whipped out his badge. He banged his palm on the window.

Jessica climbed over to the driver's side and moved the car to the opposite side of the road. She parked with the hazard lights on and watched him from afar.

"Leo, I can explain," Chelsie blurted out, holding up her hands.

"What the hell are you doing, Chelsie? Are you following me?"

"No."

Leo slammed his hand down on the roof. "Stop lying! I saw your car last night at a crime scene."

Jessica honked the horn, causing Leo and Chelsie to look in her direction.

Cheslie sneered in annoyance. "I thought you had a case to solve."

Leo pinched the bridge of his nose and bent down to glare from the window. "We are not together. I don't need to answer you."

"You lied to me! I saw you at her apartment last night."

Leo hadn't gotten the stalker vibes from her before. It felt more like persistence, showing what she wanted. Thinking back on the phone calls and food delivery once a week, he'd finally exchanged numbers and talked on the phone for a few weeks before deciding to ask her out on a date.

"Right now you're interfering with a police investigation. Lose my number, Chelsie, or you'll regret it."

Leo whirled around to leave, but Chelsie grasped his hand.

"Wait! Leo I-I'm sorry."

Leo glanced at her holding him by the wrist. "Chelsie, I have work and you are holding up traffic."

"Can't we talk about us?"

Leo snatched away. "There is no us."

"Leo! Please, Leo!" Chelsie shouted and started to open her car door when a car came barreling down the street to get around traffic.

Leo climbed back in his car and slammed the door.

"Should I be worried?"

"Not the time, Jessica."

Jessica shrugged her shoulders. "Sorry, but you just stopped traffic to talk to a girl."

Leo huffed in frustration. "That was my date."

"From last night."

Leo turned at the light and hopped on the freeway. "I think she's stalking me."

Jessica gasped, then held a hand to her chest. "Are you serious?"

"I can handle her."

Traffic picked back up and moved through the streets. Leo stared ahead and peered at Jessica in the passenger seat.

Jessica looked behind her in the seat. "What's a cop, Leo? She should have been arrested a long time ago."

"It was one date and I think she got the message. Besides, it's your fault."

Jessica pointed at her chest. "How is it my fault?"

"She thought we had something going on because I was at your place last night."

"We always go to each other's place and discuss cases."

"I know that, but she's been trying to talk to me for a

while and I finally agreed, only her first questions were pertaining to my closeness to you."

Jessica laid her hand on top of his arm. "I'm sorry, Leo."

"Yeah, I knew my job would be hard for women to take, but bringing you into it really pissed me off."

"Why?"

"Because we're friends and no one tells me who I can be friends with or date."

Jessica watched him out of the corner of her eye. "Maybe I should talk to her and let her know we are just friends."

"That will never work and besides, you will never see her again."

Jessica tilted her head. "You dumped her."

"Worry about the case."

Jessica tossed her hands up in the air. "We can talk about more than one thing, Leo, gosh."

Leo swerved into the exit lane headed to the Bengal dorm building for boys, parked immediately, turned the car off and faced Jessica.

"Chelsie and I aren't dating. It was one date."

"I hate to get in the way of you finding someone."

Leo winked at her and pushed his driver's side open. "Work is my life right now. When I'm ready to settle down, the one will come."

Chapter Eight

He checked the side of the building, waited for the last people to leave and carried the large black bag in. He kept his head down under black overalls and a hoodie, with dark shades. He clenched the doorknob, and twisted to find it open. He stalked inside of the boys' basketball changing room. Glancing around the empty lockers, he moved toward the back near the laundry bins and dumped Bonnie inside. Once she was covered up, he quickly maneuvered out when a voice called out.

"Hey, you're here late to be working out," the custodian mentioned.

He ignored him and kept walking.

"You hear me?"

He paused and raised a hand up in the air.

The janitor chuckled, pushed the mop bucket down the hall to go back to what he was working on. "You kids are always into some shit."

He started up his car and drove away feeling the intensity of what could have happened. He wanted to stop, but *felt it was too late to not feel that rush of love he'd always wanted and desired.*

He pulled back into his home in the middle of the night, shut his car off in the garage, and blew out a breath. As soon as he stepped out of the car, he felt a chill run up his spine, like someone was watching him.

He peered around the neighborhood and saw all of the lights off, cars parked. Shaking his head he headed inside and removed his shoes and his clothes. He tossed them in a garbage bag and jumped in the shower to clean up. It was going to be busy day tomorrow and he had to make sure everything went according to plan, before he brought his next treat home.

The following morning bright and early, he checked to make sure the basement was clean and dusted of Bonnie being there. He liked every girl to feel special, so he placed flowers on the side table, and placed a fresh bottle of wine in the fridge upstairs. Swiping up the car keys, he bit into an apple he'd grabbed from the kitchen, walked out of the house, and locked the front door.

"Good morning, neighbor!" The young woman waved from next door.

"Morning to you."

"Are you going to the basketball game at the college?"

"Wouldn't miss it."

He shut the door and tossed his jacket on the seat, reversed out of the driveaway and headed to Bengal College.

The roar of the crowd blared through the speakers as cheerleaders threw their hands in the air, while fans spoke about how much they're going to be the number one to beat. Banners hung around the gymnasium, as the semi-finals for the Bengal basketball team came down to the wire with ten minutes left in the game. Starting basketball player Harper Divine gripped the ball in his hand. Sweat dripped down his forehead. Squinting his eyes, he released the ball with his heart beating fast praying it hit the goal.

"AHHHH!"

The loud scream caused the entire assembly of students, teachers, and reporters to rise from their seats.

A young woman wearing a staff uniform in the Bengal colors grabbed a security officer and pointed toward the locker rooms.

"She's dead! She's dead."

"Ladies and gentlemen, please stay in your seats." The announcer spoke on the mic.

Jessica pushed through the crowd. Leo followed behind her and held up his badge to the local security.

"What's all the commotion?" Leo asked.

"They found a body in the locker room."

"A dead body."

The security guard motioned to the black doors in the back. "Yep. Through the back locker room."

"Stay here," Leo told Jessica, nodded and scanned the entire gym.

As she watched the police walk inside, she watched Harper talk with his coach. To the left of the gym, Cedric sat with Liddy, the young girl who was upset talking to Dean Chancellor.

"That's Bonnie!" one of the basketball players blurted out.

Harper and Jessica's heads whipped around at the mention of her name. Harper bolted from the sidelines to get a closer look and a crowd of police and security held him back.

"Wait! I need to see her," Harper begged, shoving a security guard back.

Jessica glanced at the body being wheeled out and rushed to Leo to get answers in the back.

"They said it's Bonnie."

Leo raked a hand on the back of his neck. "It's her."

Jessica closed her eyes and dropped her shoulders in disappointment. Her thoughts went back to her best friends being in the same situation along with herself almost being killed at the hands of a lunatic. More tears wafted through the gym as President Chancellor appeared, taking the mic to address the students.

"At this point in time, we will cancel the game."

"Boo!"

"That's not fair! We're about to win."

Yelling and shouting from each basketball staff sent up high emotions with the players and fans. Jessica moved through the locker room, watched the police interview staff and block off the area.

"What time do you think she died?"

"They said possibly around midnight," Leo answered, glared at the lockers, then up to the security cameras.

"What?"

Leo pointed to the camera up above in the corner of the exits. "Security cameras."

Jessica lifted her pen and pushed the towel away to get a clear view inside the hamper. "No witness to the body being dropped?"

"Not yet. I need to check the footage."

A security guard approached. "The camera is broken. It's supposed to be replaced next week."

"How convenient," Jessica mumbled.

Leo thanked him, shook hands and gestured to Jessica

to walk with him back to the gym floor. President Chancellor stood in front of reporters while some of the students started to leave the gym. A few held up their phones and recorded the scene.

"We are heartbroken by Bonnie's life being taken away so soon. She was a lovely student here at Bengal College."

"President Chancellor, is it true this is a pattern at Bengal College of missing students?" a local reporter suggested.

Jessica caught President Chancellor's long stare and wondered if it could be a sign of descent.

"Bengal College is a great school. Nothing about these two incidents show a pattern," President Chancellor insisted.

Jessica cleared her throat, then raised her hand in the air. "Actually, President Chancellor, you're wrong. My research shows over the past few months up to a year missing women have gone unreported."

Dean frowned. Flashes of the light from the cameras brought him out of his stare toward Jessica.

"What do you have to say to that accusation?" Another reporter insisted, shoving the mic in his face for an answer.

"Well, until the police bring the information, I can't state anything at the moment. Again, our basketball team will reschedule the game while the police handle the investigation."

"Alright everyone, time to leave out!" Leo shouted and motioned to the exit doors.

Jessica slowly walked up on Dean Chancellor as he walked out of the gymnasium. She watched him reach in his pocket to remove his cell.

"President Chancellor, I would like to speak with you privately if that's possible."

"You will need to schedule something with my assistant."

"Sir, a body was found on campus grounds and you're acting like it means nothing."

A crowd of students and faculty slowed down and gasped at her outburst.

President Chancellor peered around the hall and smiled. "Everything is fine. Please move along." He gestured to Jessica. "Fine. If you want to talk, let's go to my office."

Jessica nodded and followed.

The press disbursed. Leo stayed back and talked with the local police.

Jessica walked into President Chancellor's office and took a seat in front of his desk. Chancellor sat on the edge of his desk with his hands clasped together.

"What's your angle?"

"Angle?" Jessica quipped.

Dean Chancellor crossed his arms, stood up, and paced back and forth behind Jessica. "You've caused a lot of noise for me and I'd like for it to stop."

"Are you seriously making this about me?"

"My students are looking at leaving Bengal and transferring out because you've made it seem like a killer is running around town."

"Because there is one!" Jessica shouted.

Dean Chancellor's eyes rose in anger, and he pointed his finger in her face. "Listen to me, Jessica Smith. I know you're looking to make this story your big break, but I will bury you under so much litigation, your grandchildren will be owing us money."

"Are you threatening me?"

President Chancellor walked to the window and slipped both hands in his pocket. "This is a business at the end of the day. We have a board that we answer to and you've made my job more complicated."

Jessica rose from the seat. "If you're hiding something, it would be easier to tell me now before I find out."

Jessica picked up the pictures on his desk of his family and dog. "You have a lovely family. How is Liddy doing?" Jessica asked.

Dean froze at her question. "Who?"

Jessica shook her head. "The student I saw stopped you one day in the hall. You two seemed very close."

Dean Chancellor's eyes widened in agitation. "Are you suggesting I have a relationship with a student?"

"I never suggested, only observed how she felt comforted by your attention." Jessica knew in the back of her mind, Liddy was spotted with him and Cedric the TA and she could possibly be in danger.

A knock interrupted his response. "Come in."

Leo poked his head in and looked between Jessica and President Chancellor. "I came to talk to you about Bonnie."

Dean walked back behind his desk and took a seat. "All I know about her is that she was dating the star athlete. Have you talked with him?"

"He was at practice late, then went home and his roommate confirmed." Leo watched Jessica sternly gaze at Chancellor.

President Chancellor scratched the back of his neck.

"The pattern you brought up might help the case."

"If it gets out that kids go missing, it will ruin the school."

"Are you worried about the missing girls or your job?" Jessica checked.

Dean jumped up and gestured to Jessica. "I want her arrested for harassment!"

Jessica glanced at Leo.

"Sir, we're only here to help solve the crime. If she has information that can help, we need to listen."

Jessica bit her bottom lip. "I read over all the notes from Bonnie and Jocelyn's case and compared it to other women and they are all connected together in age range, weight, and personality."

"How so?"

"Each one broke up with a boyfriend and later went missing."

"Well, there's your answer. Arrest the boyfriend."

"Also, they have familiarity with Cedric the TA."

"Cedric, who works here? You've got to be kidding."

"How long has he worked here?"

"Long enough that I trust him."

Jessica thought to mention Cedric to see how the president would react and like she suspected, he protected him.

"Then I might be wrong."

President Chancellor picked up the phone. "Yeah, not surprised. Anything else because I have work to do with making calls to try and fix the mess you placed my school into with our board and the media."

"Thank you. We will be in touch with any follow up questions."

Jessica and Leo left his office and marched down the entry to the exits. Leo tugged his keys out of his pockets and headed to his car.

"He's lying."

"Not the first person to lie to you, Jess."

"Yeah, but I can feel it in my gut."

"Did he threaten you?"

"He tried, but he's too cowardly. I think he's sleeping with students."

Leo backed out of the parking space and turned into traffic. "They all sleep with students at one time or another. The sad thing is the students never tell."

Chapter Nine

After the body of Bonnie was discovered, Leo dropped Jessica at home while he went to the police station to handle the investigation with his team. Jessica ate and changed clothes while packing up her notes on the case. Jessica lifted her glasses and removed the case file from her lap and stood to stretch her legs and arms. Reading over three other cases of missing women at Bengal took an emotional toll, and she needed to change up her setting and decided to try the office. Jessica locked her apartment and held her phone while she waited for Leo to answer.

The door of her neighbor popped open as Adam came out of his place at the same time.

"Hey Jessica, I was going to ask if you're working that case about the college," Adam wondered.

Jessica held up a finger to pause him while she left a message. "Hey Leo, about to head to the office. Call me later."

"Crazy how you never know people."

"Scary."

"True."

The ding of the elevator let them off at the lobby floor.

"See you later, Jessica."

"You, too."

Jessica waved goodbye and walked to the mailbox in the corner of the building and unlocked it to remove a bundle of mail.

Jessica sighed. "All bills."

Jessica threw everything in her backpack and chucked her chin up at the guard on duty as he opened the door for her to leave. The sprinkling of rain annoyed her as she bumped into a body running toward the cab.

"Oh shit, sorry."

Cedric stepped to the side. "Sorry. I didn't see you there."

Jessica eyed him nervously. "You're far from the Bengal campus."

"I was meeting a friend."

"Are you dating Liddy, the girl I saw you with the other day?"

Honk!

Jessica and Cedric glanced at the cab driver.

"Is someone going to hop in or not? I have another person waiting," he grumbled.

"It's my personal business, but I am seeing her."

"Interesting. But what about Bonnie?"

"I will get the next cab."

Cedric ignored her questions and backed away. She watched him as the rain started to get heavier.

Jessica climbed into the car and shut the door. She stared at Cedric as he stuck a hand out for the next cab.

Ring!

Jessica stretched her hand in her pocket to lift her phone. "Leo."

"I got your message. Still at the station."

Jessica whipped out a napkin to dry off a little from the rain as she headed to work. "I am on my way to the office to get some work done."

"Do you need me to pick you up?"

"Won't your girlfriend think that's weird?" Jessica teased, ready to find out more about his dating life with Chelsie. Between the both of them it was embarrassing neither really kept up with the people in their personal lives.

Leo groaned. "Whatever, Jess. Call me later-"

"Wait! Cedric."

"What about him?"

"He bumped into me."

Leo scrunched up his face. "When?"

"Just now when I was getting into my cab."

"Are you hurt? He try anything?"

Jessica caught the eye of the cab driver, then covered her mouth as she talked in the phone. "No, it was harmless. I found out he's seeing Liddy."

"The girl you mentioned to Dean."

Jesscia switched the phone from left to right. "Yes, so can you follow up with her?"

"Writing it down now."

"Thanks, Leo."

"Stay safe and call me later." Leo finished talking and hung up.

"Here you are at the newspaper office. Are you a reporter or something?" the cabbie asked.

Jessica counted out fifty dollars and passed the bills to him. "I am."

"So you're like Barbara Walters or something."

"Not that major." Jessica chuckled.

He turned his head to face her in the backseat. "You should write about me."

"Maybe next time." Jessica shoved the door open, slammed it shut and ran to get inside to dry off.

Jessica snatched up the latest paper on the rack near the elevator and carried it up to the main floor and lifted a cup to pour coffee from the break room. She walked to her office, saw a few friends and waved as she unlocked her office door. She removed her jacket and tossed her backpack on the couch. Jessica placed the coffee down on the desk and walked to the bathroom. She turned the light on and grabbed the towel on the wall to dry off.

Ellen ambled in and stood at the bathroom entry. "Knock, knock."

Jessica wiped her arms and neck down.

"You're soaked."

"I got caught up in the rain."

"How is the case coming along?"

Jessica followed her editor from the bathroom and took a seat at her desk, picked up the coffee and sipped.

"A few leads, and now that Bonnie's body was found they're ramping up the search."

"Good news."

"I hate that she wasn't found in time. More girls are suffering."

"Sad all around, but we need to get as much information out to the public."

Jessica waved to the couch. "Can you bring me my backpack?"

Ellen turned and bent down to pick it up from the couch.

"Thanks. I ran through case files and matched up that all the girls are around twenty-one to twenty-four. Each one came in contact with three men."

Her brows lifted in concern. "Three men."

Jessica grabbed her notepad and case files, then flipped them open. "Look at the photos of each girl. They're around the same height, weight, and ages."

"So a total of six girls over a year, and the last two turned up dead fairly close in time."

"Which tells me he got scared."

"Why?"

"Maybe the media attention."

"Possibly the media, but it could be that you've made it fairly public with being on campus non-stop since you got on the case."

Jessica sat back in her chair. "You think it's me."

"The first four girls went missing without any awareness and died at least two to four months apart except the last two."

"He knows we're onto him."

"I think another girl is going to go missing."

"Any clues?"

Jessica exhaled a breath. "Liddy."

"Liddy."

"I think it is the TA and he's dating her."

Ellen leaned against the desk. "Did you tell Leo?"

"Before I came here I bumped into the guy named Cedric that works at the school, and somehow he comes up either with the crowd or near my apartment."

Ellen's brow knitted together in confusion. "He's stalking you?"

"I can't say for sure."

Ellen dropped her head back, stared at the ceiling. "Jesus, Jessica, you need to be careful."

"Believe me. I know, but we can't really arrest him because he hasn't done anything."

"Publicly."

"Exactly."

"Well, type up what you have and send it over to me. I really want to wrap the story up sooner than later."

Ellen liked to have the story ahead of time and Jessica was known for being last minute with the deadline.

Jessica flopped down in her chair and logged in her computer. "I will."

Ellen stood at the door with her hand on the knob. "And get some security in case you need the backup."

"I was thinking of going to the campus after I'm done writing up my notes."

"That might be dangerous, Jessica. Should I send someone with you?"

Jessica's stomach grumbled. She pulled the drawer open and picked up a candy bar. "Still daytime. Nothing will happen. The campus is full of people."

"Alright, but call me if you need me."

Jessica saluted her and turned to her computer and started inputting every detail from her notepad. She stared at each photo and shook her head. "We're going to get justice for you all. I promise."

Jessica dropped the pictures, bypassed the title *Missing Girls of Bengal College* and continued typing out each paragraph of details from their birth all the way up to what they were studying in school.

* * *

Finally back on campus, Jessica moved around the athletes who came in and out of the locker room when she spotted Bonnie's ex-boyfriend making out with another woman.

"Excuse me," Jessica muttered.

He split apart from his girlfriend. "What are you doing back here?"

"I came to apologize."

Her head reared back. "Apologize?" the short blonde, brown eyed girl asked.

"I thought he killed Bonnie, but I know that he didn't."

"Killed Bonnie!" she shouted and he glared at Jessica.

"Are you crazy? You shouldn't be in here."

"What is she talking about killing Bonnie?"

Jessica gestured her hand in between them. "Oh no, I was wrong. See, we were in her old dorm room together." Jessica continued to make suggestions that put him in a bad mood.

"Babe, what is she going on about?"

He frowned and balled his fists. "Nothing. She's crazy."

"Oh, sorry, didn't mean to make you feel uncomfortable. He's a great guy. Bonnie thought so, but that's how she turned out."

Harper took a step and his girl pulled him back by his arm. "I had nothing to do with Bonnie's death, bitch!"

Jessica folded her arms. "Prove it," she demanded.

She waited for him to break his stare off.

"Bonnie wanted to study and I was planning on breaking up with her at the cafe. She was too worried about her passing her final."

"Final exams," Jessica muttered.

He reached for his date's hand and started to walk away. "Leave me alone, or else, I will have my father put a restraining order on you."

Jessica held a perplexed look in her eye, then walked through the exits of the gym and out to her car. She took out her keys to unlock the car and hopped inside. "Her studies," she mumbled.

Pop!

Jessica turned her head, cupped the back of her neck, and felt blood trail down as her eyes became blurry. "What the hell?" Jessica muttered.

Chelsie shoved Jessica in her car. She picked up her cell and threw it out of the window and she drove away from campus. "We need to chat."

Thirty minutes later, Jessica slowly woke up still groggy and her vision was blurry. What came into focus was a woman holding a gun.

"Sleeping beauty has woken up."

"Who are you?"

"Someone that can make your life either good or bad, so don't piss me off."

Jessica scanned the modest office and tried to sit up, but her hands and legs were tied together. "Listen, I can get you money."

Chelsie cackled. "Money is the last thing you could offer me. There is something more important you can do for me though."

Jessica gulped.

"Finally have the chance to meet the infamous Jessica Smith and she's not what I thought you'd be."

"I-I-I don't understand," Jessica stammered.

"Relax, we have plenty of time to catch up. Until my husband gets here."

Jessica twisted her wrist trying to get out of the ropes. "Husband."

Chelsie held the phone in her hands, turned her back on Jessica and dialed his number. Falling in love with him was unexpected, and she tried her best to get him to see her as the woman of his dreams. Every chance they talked he'd bring up Jessica Smith and she wondered how close they were to each other. He'd told her about them being long-time friends, but Chelsie could see the look in his eyes when her name was spoken. No matter how long she brought him lunch at work or called to check on him throughout the day, he'd blown off her advances until finally they had dinner. She'd started to break his walls down until she'd become too possessive. In her mind Leo loved her, but Jessica was holding him back and needed to be removed from his life. Then he could fully love her the way she loves him.

"Please, I don't know who your husband is, but I can promise I've never spoken to him."

Chelsie turned. She stalked over to Jessica, raised her hand and back slapped her.

"Shut up!" Frustrated that Leo hadn't picked up her call, Chelise paced back and forth gripping the gun tightly.

Chapter Ten

As Leo came from the bathroom at the precinct, he adjusted his badge. He glanced up at the clock on the wall to see the time. A fellow officer flagged him down before he could sit. "Leo, listen to this story."

Leo noticed the young woman shivering under a blanket with tears falling down her cheeks.

"What's going on, Steward?"

"Tell me again what happened. You can trust him." Steward spoke gently to the young lady.

Alyssa pushed her hair behind her ear and wiped her nose on the tissue. "I had a paper due and thought I could get some extra help from my professor."

"You are Alyssa Simmons right? Jocelyn's friend," Leo remembered.

"Yes," Alyssa muttered.

Steward reached for the tissue box on his desk. "Take deep breaths and start from the beginning."

Alyssa shut her eyes and blew out a breath. "He tried to kill me."

Leo pulled a chair close to her. "Who?"

"Professor Williams."

Leo and Steward stared at each other in surprise.

"At Bengal College."

"Yes, I went to his office and overheard him talking, but it sounded like he was really angry. I think something broke. I started to walk away when the door opened and he had this angry look on his face."

"Was anyone else around?"

Alyssa wiped the tear from her cheek. "No, I barely got away."

"Where did he take you?"

Her lips trembled. "To his house."

"Then what happened?"

"He tried to throw me in the basement and I fought him really hard and ran out of there."

"Anything else you can think about maybe? Something that stuck out to you?"

"He kept rambling on about how they never stay. She made him do it."

"She made him do it?"

Alyssa gulped down the bottle of water. "His house was wrecked and a few newspapers were scattered around. A lot of it mentioned that lady, Jessica Smith."

"Thank you, Alyssa. Steward will get you to the hospital to get checked out."

"Can I call my mom?" Alyssa wondered.

Leo stood up and moved up to the corner of the hallway. "Yes, of course. Steward, let me talk to you for a second."

"What are you thinking?"

"We have our guy and need to get him right now before he tries to take another girl."

"She's the only one that can identify him."

"Need to keep her under protection. I don't care how much the captain bitches and moans."

"I got you, but where are you going?"

"Jessica could be in trouble."

"She wouldn't be anywhere near his palace."

"You don't know Jessica Smith like I do."

Leo snatched up his keys and jogged out of the station. He hopped in his car, hit Bluetooth to connect to Jessica's phone and like always, it went straight to voicemail.

"Come on, Jessica, answer the phone. No time to play around."

He ended the call and started to dial again when he looked in the rearview mirror and noticed a car following him.

Leo swerved at the stoplight and listened to the other car honking their horn. "She's really trying my patience." He picked up speed down the block to get away, when the car came up following him again. While he paid attention to the phone dialing, he quickly made a turn at the light, hung up on Jessica and called Steward to grab the address.

"I have people dispatched." Steward mentioned it as soon as the call connected.

"I got someone following me. Can you get someone to Jessica's apartment and check to see if she's alright?"

"Who's following you?"

"Chelsie."

"Wait, Chelsie the paralegal?"

Leo rolled his eyes. "Steward, focus. Chelsie is a long story. Just make sure Jessica has someone at her place."

"Alright and Professor Williams lives alone. Digging

through his background, he was arrested years ago for domestic violence."

"How the hell did he get a job at Bengal College?"

"Seems President Dean Chancellor and Professor Williams are old friends," Steward expressed.

"Great, more secrets and find Dean Chancellor. I don't trust him at all."

"Backup should be there by the time you make it to his place."

Leo gazed down to check the time on the radio. "Should be there in about ten minutes."

"Don't do anything crazy."

Leo dragged a hand down his face and slowed down at the stop sign one block from Professor Williams' home. "Tell that to Williams and Chancellor."

He tapped his finger on the steering wheel, glanced in the side mirror and saw Chelsie's car was no longer following him.

"Crazy bitch."

Leo drove off and slowly arrived at a house down from Professor Williams. He pulled his gun to check and badge before getting out of the car. Leo pushed the driver's side open and shut behind him as two patrol cars stopped beside him. He moved to the window and dipped his head to speak.

"No eyes on the inside. The girl said it was empty when she escaped."

"You want us in the back," the officer asked.

Leo peered up at the house and pointed. "Two of you with me and the other two in the back."

Going on seven at night, all the men jogged up to the house. It was dimly lit with no car in sight. Leo cocked his head up to continue moving forward as he held his gun.

He held up three fingers and counted down. He lifted his leg and kicked the door down and startled Professor Williams as he came out of the kitchen holding a knife in his hand.

"Put the knife down and step back," Leo demanded.

"What the hell is going on?"

"Professor Williams, you have the right to remain silent."

The rest of the team came in from the back door, as Leo watched Professor Williams be handcuffed. Leo tilted his head to confirm with his team they had the situation under control while he moved toward searching the home.

"I haven't done anything wrong!" Professor Williams shouted.

"Leo, I think you might want to see downstairs," an officer called out.

"You can't go down there. I know my rights." Professor Williams squirmed on the ground.

"Alyssa Simmons came to the police station tonight and stated you kidnapped and tried to kill her, but she escaped," Leo spoke.

Professor Williams became quiet.

Leo stalked down the hall to the door at the far off corner of the kitchen, grabbed the light and peered at the pictures on the wall of women from Bengal College, leading down the stairs to a basement filled with a fridge, couch, table, and clothes on a rack.

"Are you getting everything? Make sure you get pictures."

Leo waved at each wall filled with pictures from each missing woman from Bengal. Leo grabbed the gloves from a fellow officer and opened the fridge. A stack of vials lined up with blood labeled by each girl's name.

"Shit, he's got at least six vials here."

"The same amount of girls who are missing."

Leo flicked through a few newspaper articles on the table of everything that had been talked about with the case.

A cop jogged downstairs. "Leo, you need to come up here."

Leo walked to the bottom of the stairs. "Something else he's hiding?"

"It is Jesscia."

Leo brows furrowed. "She's alright?"

"She wasn't at her place when they went to check on her."

Leo bolted up the stairs and tugged on his phone from his holster. "What about her office?"

As he sprinted through the house his line of sight moved toward Professor Williams being questioned, more police moving in and out of the house. Neighbors walked outside as he clamored down the stairs.

"Is Professor Williams alright?" an older woman with her husband asked.

"Ma'am, we need everybody to stay back," a cop demanded.

* * *

Leo ignored them and listened to Jessica's voicemail pop on. "Jessica, call me back ASAP." He ran to his car and jumped in. He put it in drive and zoomed out of the area, driving back to her place.

As soon as Leo came up to downtown Manhattan near her offices his phone rang.

"Hey Leo, this is her editor. I was calling because she never returned my call from earlier."

"Did she say where she was going?"

"To find some more details at the college and then home."

"Yeah and my men said they haven't seen her at her place."

"That's strange."

Beep!

Leo moved the phone from his ear seeing unknown number. "Hold on for a second. I got another call."

"Sure."

"This is Leo."

"She's pretty, Leo."

Leo sucked in a shaky breath. "Chelsie."

She giggled. "I told her you thought it would be a good job to let her down easy."

"Chelsie, is Jessica with you?"

"Leo!" Jessica screamed.

"Shut up, bitch," Chelsie snapped.

Leo squinted his eyes, his heart pounding in his chest. "Where are you at, Chelsie?"

"Well, since you bailed out on me, and missed coming home with me," Chelsie cooed through the phone.

Leo bit his bottom lip, then opened and closed his fist to control his temper. "Chelsie, listen to me."

"No, you listen. Jessica is the only thing keeping us apart," Chelsie barked.

Leo slapped his hand on his thigh, frustrated that his personal life caught up with his friend. "It was one date, Chelsie--"

"That's a lie!"

"Okay, okay. Tell me where you are."

"I almost caught you tonight."

"Caught me? That was you following me again?"

She laughed. "I think you really forgot how much I care for you, Leo."

Leo moved the phone from his ear and slapped his hand against the steering wheel. "Chelsie, we can talk together. Just let Jessica go."

"Promise me something, Leo."

"Chelsie, if you hurt her..."

The thought of someone hurting Jessica because of him was a long time fear he held to his chest.

"Are you threatening me, Leo?"

Leo squeezed his eyes shut. "No, Chelsie. I can get to you in less than a minute."

"Meet me where our first date was."

"The restaurant."

"No, my office."

Rain started to pour down as Leo swiftly headed through traffic. "On my way."

"See you soon, baby."

Leo listened to the dial tone, dropped his head back on the seat and called for backup. "Steward, I need backup at Don Langley Law Firm."

"Is it Jessica?"

"Chelsie kidnapped her and is holding her."

"Shit, on my way man."

"Get Don on the phone and find out everything you can about Chelsie."

"Leo, be careful, and wait for us to get to you. Chelsie is probably setting you up."

Honk!

A bus drove through the light almost hitting his bumper as Leo sharply moved to the right lane and pushed the pedal down and sped to the offices where Chelsie worked.

"I met her the first time when I was working on a case and from then on, she's come to the police station almost weekly."

"She's obsessed, man."

"Same as Professor Williams," Leo mentioned and parked directly in front of the firm's building. He hopped out holding his phone.

"I got people on their way."

"I'm going in now."

"Leo, wait-"

He disconnected the call and ran up the stairs of the law offices and banged on the door, getting the attention of the security team.

Leo snatched his badge off his hip and placed it in the window. The guard waved him off and Leo pounded again on the door.

The security guard stood from his desk, rolled his eyes, and marched to the door. "We're closed, man."

Leo banged his hand on the window. "I need to get inside. It's a police emergency."

The bulky security guard blew a breath and clasped a hand around the lock to speak. "I said we are closed."

"Has anyone come up here in the last hour?"

"Man, are you crazy? Everybody is gone for the night."

Leo pushed his way through the lobby door and jogged around the desk to glance at the security cameras. Time moves fast when dealing with unstable people holding someone you care about in a harmful situation.

"What about your security cameras?"

"I've been here all night and nothing has gotten by me."

"Can you rewind the tapes? What about the back exits?"

"No one comes from the back unless it's the cleaning service taking out some trash."

The sounds of police sirens blasting outside caused them both to look up.

"Aye, what's going on?"

"Someone's been kidnapped and possibly brought here. I need the entire place shut down and all exits covered." Leo snatched the walkie-talkie off the desk.

"That's mine!" the guard yelled.

Leo grasped him around the neck and pushed him against the wall. "If anything happens to my friend because of your incompetence, I will kill you myself."

Steward walked up on him and clapped a hand on his shoulder. "Leo, back up."

He rubbed his neck as Leo let him go. "He's crazy."

Steward cocked his head to the side, pointed a finger in his face. "Are you going to be able to handle what we walk in on or do I need to take the lead? I know she means a lot to you."

"I can handle it. Let's go." Leo marched through the lobby and up the stairs. He remembered Chelsie's floor number. A gang of police officers followed them as Steward directed a few to stay behind and cover the exits. Leo removed his gun and some went to the back area of the building.

Leo sauntered to the front offices of Don Langley Law Offices. "Hello, I'm Detective Leo Walsh. I need to speak with your boss."

"May I ask what this is in regards to, Detective?"

Leo bent down to stare into her eyes. "You can ask me anything, Chelsie Banks."

She grinned, licked her bottom lip, and picked up the phone to buzz her boss's office. "Make sure to not be a stranger, Detective Walsh."

Leo winked at her, walked around desk and headed to Don's office.

That day was the worst day in his life thinking back on the first time he met Chelsie. He thought about the look in her eyes and wanting more just from the subtle hints.

Steward stuck two fingers up in the air, tilted to the right and left side of the main floor. Leo chucked his head up in the air confirming to move in first with backup next to him. Slowly they walked down the empty hall and checked each closed door for any suspicious activity.

"He doesn't love you!" Cheslie screamed.

"You need help, Chelsie," Jessica replied.

Leo pointed toward the direction of the loud voices and picked up their pace.

"On three," Steward whispered.

Leo mouthed, "One. Two. Three."

Steward gently pushed the door open. The sound caused Chelsie to grip Jessica by the arm and hold a gun to her head.

"Back up or I will kill her."

Jessica glanced from Steward to Leo along with the police holding guns in their direction.

Chelsie tightened her grip on her arm. "Leo, I told you to come alone. We have a lot to discuss."

Leo's breathing was heavy. He squinted his eyes and closed in on Chelsie and Jessica. "Chelsie, let her go."

"She doesn't deserve you! I can make you happy," she shouted.

Jessica shook her head to not come any closer. Chelsie had gone off the deep end with her obsession with Leo. The feelings that Chelise was displaying reminded her of what Bonnie, Jocelyn, and the other women went through.

"We can talk as soon as you let her go."

Chelsie scanned the other policemen in the back. "Tell them to leave."

"Okay, just put the gun down."

"No! I only want to talk to you."

"Alright! Jessica, are you hurt?"

"I'm fine."

Chelsie yanked her by the back of her head, as her hand with the other gun went down. "Why are you asking about this bitch!"

Leo charged at her and grabbed her wrist as Jessica bumped Chelsie with the back of her elbow.

Cheslie fell on top of the desk as Leo hovered over her body. "I hate you!"

"Jessica, you good?"

Steward approached and helped her stand up.

Chelsie begged, tears pooled into her eyes. "Leo, I love you so much. Just give us a chance."

"Chelsie, you have the right to remain silent."

"No! I want to talk to you."

Steward hauled her off in handcuffs.

Leo stretched his arms around Jessica and checked over her face and body. "Are you hurt?"

"How many times are you going to save me before I have to return the favor?"

He chuckled. "Too many to count."

"We need to get to Professor Williams' house."

"He's in police custody."

Jessica and Leo walked out of the office and down to the elevator. "You got him."

Leo picked up a blanket and wrapped it around her shoulders next to the ambulance. "Yeah, Alyssa came into the police station after running away. I was calling you, but got no answer and sent some men to find you."

"I was leaving Bengal Campus when I got knocked over the head and confronted by your girlfriend." Jessica let the EMT check her out on the gurney.

"Is she going to be alright?"

"We'd like to bring you in for a follow up, but nothing stands out," the EMT explained.

"He's bossy. I am fine, Leo."

"Don't listen to her."

"Leo! Leo, please tell them you love me," Chelsie shouted as policemen put her in the back of the squad car.

"Kind of ironic."

Leo peered at her. "What is ironic?"

"Professor Williams and Chelsie both went off my radar as being crazy. I thought it was Cedric the TA or Dean Chancellor."

Leo climbed up on the ambulance as the doors closed. "We can talk once you are checked out."

Jessica laid back on the bed, extended her hand for Leo to take and squeezed.

"Thank you for coming to my rescue."

"We're friends. You can't get rid of me."

The sirens of the ambulance turned on as they weaved in and out of traffic.

"Best friends."

Leo winked. "Best friends."

* * *

A week later Leo pounded on the front door of Jessica's apartment, holding two cups of coffee and a cheese and egg bagel sandwich for breakfast. After waiting five minutes, the locks clicked and she appeared with a smile on her face.

Leo laughed, stepping into her apartment. "Morning, sunshine."

"I hope you have French toast and sausages in there."

"Have they had the press conference yet?"

Jessica lifted the vanilla latte from the tray, took a sip and plopped down on the couch. She pulled the bag of breakfast goodness open. "About to start now."

Leo handed her napkin and fork. "Here, you want some syrup?"

"Shush, it's about to start."

"We have breaking news, as Dean Chancellor comes out to the podium and gives a brief detail of what has gone on at Bengal College."

President Chancellor stared straight into the camera. "After further investigation and working with the police, we have terminated Professor Williams from his duties. I want to extend a prayer to each of the family members that were hurt."

"What do you say about your position with a call from the board for you to submit your resignation after a relationship with a student was found out?" a reporter yelled.

Jessica reached for the remote and turned up the sound. "Oh my god!"

Dean glared at the reporter. "My personal relationship has nothing to do with my job. I had a platonic adult relationship, but I have given my resignation to the board so as not to distract from the trust that needs to be built."

"I knew it."

"Liddy must have come forward."

"Hopefully more girls will speak up."

Leo snatched the remote from her lap and changed the channel. "Let us eat and watch something else until I need to get to work."

Jesscia laid her head on the back of the couch and exhaled. "I have a vacation for a week. Are you planning on babysitting me the whole time?"

"Yep, you are a hothead constantly getting into crazy situations. Someone has to watch your back."

Jessica laughed and gently punched him on the arm. "Shut up."

"You know I am right."

Jessica stuck her tongue out mockingly as they continued to talk and laugh while watching an old episode of *Murder, She Wrote*.

"Ohh, I love this show."

"I wonder why." Leo smirked.

* * *

I hope you enjoyed Jessica's story in the latest installment. Please also check out **"Mirror of Murder (A Jessica Smith Mystery) Book 4" coming soon.** Also, if you love Thriller, Mystery, Suspense check out **Agent Red: Fatal Memory Book 1 here** . Another thriller, crime fiction **"Ruined" here** https://books2read.com/u/bzVGAj

Check out free short here ***"The Firm"*** https://payhip.com/b/py7S

Grab Boxset "**Agent Red 1-3**" here https://payhip.com/b/1KcxY

Reading Order of Agent Red Series

1. Fatal Memory

https://books2read.com/u/4j2PYX

2.Fatal Target
https://books2read.com/u/bWP8Jq

3.Fatal Crime
https://books2read.com/u/mZadZJ

5.Fatal Enemy
https://books2read.com/u/bxeo1q

6. Fatal Death
https://books2read.com/u/mqwlRv

7. Fatal Pursuit
https://books2read.com/u/3JnKyA

8. **Fatal Revenge**
https://books2read.com/u/bOPowo

9. **Fatal Attack**
https://books2read.com/u/bwwKWP

Reading Order of Mirror Series

Mirror of Lies Book 1
https://books2read.com/u/mgjEPx

Mirror of Lust Book 2
https://books2read.com/u/mVRpz2

Mirror of Danger Book 3

https://books2read.com/u/b5z8o1

Mirror of Murder Book 4

Mirror of Escape Book 5

What's Next?

Want to know what happens next? Follow me at the links below to catch the next release.

Thank you so much for reading, and if you enjoyed the crazy ride and decided to leave a review, we'd truly appreciate the support. Reviews are the lifeblood of the publishing world. They're read, appreciated, and needed. Please consider taking the time to leave a few words on Goodreads or BookBub.

Sign up for updates and sneak peeks at the sites below:

www.authoravasking.com
www.bookbub.com/avasking
www.goodreads.com/author/avasking
www.Twitter.com/authoravaking
www.Instagram.com/authoravasking
www.Facebook.com/authoravasking
www.304publishing.tumblr.com

Acknowledgments

I want to thank my team, who helps me behind the scenes, from my editors to my test readers and graphic designers, and the list goes on. I truly appreciate each of you for keeping me on my toes.

About the Author

Ava S. King is the debut author of thriller, mystery, suspense, and psychological crime novels.

If you want to know when the next book will come out, please visit Author Ava S.King website at http://www.authoravasking.com, where you can sign up to receive an email for her next release.

About 304 Publishing Company

We showcase authors writing African American, interracial, women's fiction, urban romance, erotica, and contemporary romance novels, along with thrillers, suspense novels, poetry collections, and beauty & style books.www.304publishing.com

Join our mailing list to stay updated with new releases and blog posts.